MW01136419

AREA OF INFLUENCE

MANDY M. ROTH

Area of Influence© 2017, Mandy M. Roth

ALL RIGHTS RESERVED.

All books copyrighted to the author and may not be resold or given away without written permission from the author, Mandy M. Roth.

This novel is a work of fiction. Any and all characters, events, and places are of the author's imagination and should not be confused with fact. Any resemblance to persons, living or dead, or events or places is merely coincidence. Novel intended for adults only. Must be 18 years or older to read.

Published by Raven Happy Hour, LLC

www.ravenhappyhour.com

Raven Books and all affiliate sites and projects are © Copyrighted 2004-2017

Suggested Reading Order of Books
Released to Date in the Immortal Ops
Series World

**This list is NOT up to date. Please check
MandyRoth.com for the most current
release list.**

Suggested reading order of books released to date
in the
Immortal Ops Series world
Immortal Ops
Critical Intelligence
Radar Deception
Strategic Vulnerability
Tactical Magik
Act of Mercy
Administrative Control
Act of Surrender
Broken Communication

Separation Zone

Act of Submission

Damage Report

Act of Command

Wolf's Surrender

The Dragon Shifter's Duty

Midnight Echoes

Isolated Maneuver

Expecting Darkness

Area of Influence

More to come (check www.mandyroth.com for new releases)

Books in each series within the Immortal Ops World.
This list is NOT up to date. To see an updated list of the books within each series under the umbrella of the Immortal Ops World please visit MandyRoth.com. Mandy is always releasing new books within the series world. Sign up for her newsletter at MandyRoth.com to never miss a new release.

You can read each individual series within the world, in whatever order you want…

PSI-Ops:

Act of Mercy
Act of Surrender
Act of Submission
Act of Command
Act of Passion
And more (see Mandy's website & sign up for her
newsletter for notification of releases)

Immortal Ops:

Immortal Ops
Critical Intelligence
Radar Deception
Strategic Vulnerability
Tactical Magik
Administrative Control
Separation Zone
Area of Influence
And more…
(see Mandy's website & sign up for her newsletter
for notification of releases)

Immortal Outcasts:

Broken Communication
Damage Report
Isolated Maneuver
And more…
(see Mandy's website & sign up for her newsletter
for notification of releases)

Shadow Agents:

Wolf's Surrender
The Dragon Shifter's Duty
And more…
(see Mandy's website & sign up for her newsletter
for notification of releases)

Crimson Ops Series:

Midnight Echoes
Expecting Darkness
And more…
(see Mandy's website & sign up for her newsletter
for notification of releases)

Paranormal Regulators Series and Clear Sight Division Operatives (Part of the Immortal Ops World) Coming Soon!

Praise for Mandy M. Roth's Immortal Ops World

Silver Star Award—*I feel Immortal Ops deserves a Silver Star Award as this book was so flawlessly written with elements of intrigue, suspense and some scorching hot scenes* —Aggie Tsirikas—Just Erotic Romance Reviews

5 Stars—*Immortal Ops is a fascinating short story. The characters just seem to jump out at you. Ms. Roth wrote the main and secondary characters with such depth of emotions and heartfelt compassion I found myself really caring for them* —Susan Holly—Just Erotic Romance Reviews

Immortal Ops packs the action of a Hollywood thriller with the smoldering heat that readers can expect from Ms. Roth.

Put it on your hot list…and keep it there! —The Road to Romance

5 Stars—*Her characters are so realistic, I find myself wondering about the fine line between fact and fiction…This was one captivating tale that I did not want to end. Just the right touch of humor endeared these characters to me even more* —eCataRomance Reviews

5 Steamy Cups of Coffee—*Combining the world of secret government operations with mythical creatures as if they were an everyday thing, she (Ms. Roth) then has the audacity to make you actually believe it and wonder if there could be some truth to it. I know I did. Nora Roberts once told me that there are some people who are good writers and some who are good storytellers, but the best is a combination of both and I believe Ms. Roth is just that. Mandy Roth never fails to surpass herself*—coffeetimeromance

Mandy Roth kicks ass in this story—inthelibraryreview

Immortal Ops (I-Ops) Team Members

Lukian Vlakhusha: Alpha-Dog-One. Team captain, werewolf, King of the Lycans. Book: Immortal Ops (Immortal Ops)

Geoffroi (Roi) Majors: Alpha-Dog-Two. Second-in-command, werewolf, blood-bound brother to Lukian. Book: Critical Intelligence (Immortal Ops)

Doctor Thaddeus Green: Bravo-Dog-One. Scientist, tech guru, werepanther. Book: Radar Deception (Immortal Ops)

Jonathon (Jon) Reynell: Bravo-Dog-Two. Sniper, weretiger. Book: Separation Zone (Immortal Ops)

Wilson Rousseau: Bravo-Dog-Three. Resident smart-ass, wererat. Book: Strategic Vulnerability (Immortal Ops)

Eadan Daly: Alpha-Dog-Three. PSI-Op and

handler on loan to the I-Ops to round out the team, Fae. Book: Tactical Magik (Immortal Ops)

Lance Toov: Werepanther and vampire hybrid. Book: Area of Influence (Immortal Ops)

Colonel Asher Brooks: Chief of Operations and point person for the Immortal Ops Team. Book: Administrative Control (Immortal Ops)

Paranormal Security and Intelligence (PSI) Operatives

General Jack C. Newman: Director of Operations for PSI North American Division, werelion. Adoptive father of Missy Carter-Majors

Duke Marlow: PSI-Operative, werewolf. Book: Act of Mercy (PSI-Ops)

Doctor James (Jimmy) Hagen: PSI-Operative, werewolf. Took a ten-year hiatus from PSI. Book: Act of Surrender (PSI-Ops)

Striker (Dougal) McCracken: PSI-Operative, werewolf

Miles (Boomer) Walsh: PSI-Operative, werepanther. Book: Act of Submission (PSI-Ops)

Captain Corbin Jones: Operations coordinator and captain for PSI-Ops Team Five, werelion. Book: Act of Command (PSI-Ops)

Malik (Tut) Nasser: PSI-Operative, (PSI-Ops)

Colonel Ulric Lovett: Director of Operations, PSI-London Division

Dr. Sambora: PSI-Operative, (PSI-Ops)

Immortal Outcasts

Casey Black: I-Ops test subject, werewolf. Book: Broken Communication

Weston Carol: I-Ops test subject, werebear. Book: Damage Report

Bane Antonov: I-Ops test subject, weregorilla. Book: Isolated Maneuver

Shadow Agents

Bradley Durant: PSI-Ops: Shadow Agent Division, werewolf. Book: Wolf's Surrender

Ezra: PSI-Ops: Shadow Agent Division, dragonshifter

Caesar: PSI-Ops: Shadow Agent Division, werewolf

Crimson Sentinel Ops Division

Bhaltair: Crimson-Ops: Fang Gang, vampire. Book: Midnight Echoes

Labrainn: Crimson-Ops: Fang Gang, vampire

Auberi Bouchard: Crimson-Ops: Fang Gang, vampire

Searc Macleod: Crimson-Ops: Fang Gang, vampire. Book: Expecting Darkness

Daniel Townsend: Crimson-Ops: Fang Gang, vampire

Blaise Regnier: Crimson-Ops: Fang Gang, vampire

Paranormal Regulators

Stamatis Emathia: Paranormal Regulator, vampire

Whitney: Paranormal Regulator, werewolf

Cormag Buchanan: Paranormal Regulator, master vampire

Erik: Paranormal Regulator, shifter

Shane: Paranormal Regulator, shifter

Miscellaneous

Culann of the Council: Father to Kimberly; Badass Fae

Pierre Molyneux: Master vampire bent on creating a race of super soldiers

Gisbert Krauss: Mad scientist who wants to create a master race of supernaturals

Walter Helmuth: Head of Seattle's paranormal underground. In league with Molyneux and Krauss

Dr. Lakeland Matthews: Scientist, vital role in the creation of a successful Immortal Ops Team. Father to Peren Matthews

Dr. Bertrand: Mad scientist with Donavon Dynamics Corporation (The Corporation)

Blurb

Area of Influence

Immortal Ops Series Book Eight

Once a proud, fierce, alpha-male shifting operative with the Immortal Ops, Lance Toov finds himself under the thumb of an evil master vampire. Now a plaything, a god-like toy, he struggles with the tasks assigned to him. As his mind begins to break through the master vampire's influence, a woman comes along who changes all the rules, and ups the stakes in the most interesting of ways. Is she his salvation or will she be his downfall?

Chapter One

THOR CAME AWAKE WITH A START. One name stuck on a loop in his mind as he sat in total darkness, his breathing fast, his pulse speeding. Disoriented, he wasn't sure where he was or what had happened. It took a full minute to realize he'd been dreaming. The smell of gunfire filled his nostrils, and for a split second, he thought it was real—that someone had shot at him or near him, and that had been what had woken him from a deep sleep. The smell vanished, and he realized he'd dreamt it.

Lance.

Try as he might, the name wouldn't leave his head. It was as if his mind were a broken record and the needle was there, trapped on one word. One name that haunted him.

Lance.

Lance.

Lance.

The loop repeated again and again in his head, like a broken record, until he was on the verge of screaming. Finally, it stopped, but it didn't take with it the unease he still felt. It didn't lessen the rate at which his heart was pounding, or take with it the sense that he should run. It didn't matter that the destination was unknown to him. He caught another distant trace of gunfire, and for a second, an image of a man with an automatic weapon aimed right at him flashed through his mind. Somehow, he knew the man, but he had no name to go with the face.

"Brother," he said, though he felt no real connection to the man. What he did know was the man had been about to shoot at him—relation be damned.

As quickly as the flash in his mind came, it went, leaving the faintest of echoes remaining. His mind had become the enemy as of late. It was always playing tricks on him, even in his waking hours. There were days he questioned his sanity, and he wondered if those around him had begun to do so as well.

Tossing the sweat-soaked sheets aside, he let out a long, slow breath, doing his best to calm down. He couldn't recall the details of the dream—he never could. That hadn't stopped the dreams, or rather nightmares, from happening to him nearly daily anymore. He disliked going to sleep, hating the way he felt upon waking each night.

Panicked.

Lost.

In pain.

Confused.

His body ached as if someone had taken a bat to him. It hurt to draw in a deep breath, but he didn't know why. He wasn't injured. At least not physically. Mentally, he wasn't so sure. He did know that he'd not been attacked, yet his body felt as if he'd been through a war and emerged from the other side the loser.

Absently, he rubbed his chest, coming away with sweat before moving his hand lower, to his chiseled abs. Whenever he was stressed or felt the need to feed, he channeled the energy into working out. It meant his body was perfectly honed.

A beautiful weapon.

That was what the master, Pierre Molyneux, had taken to calling him. From the first moment he could remember, Thor had been gifted in the art of fighting and weaponry. Like he'd been born that way. He'd woken a super soldier, able to handle himself in nearly any situation. He didn't know what kind of life he'd led prior to his conversion, but since he'd been reborn part vampire, he'd been used as a weapon.

And he hated it.

Hated the way he was treated like property. Like he was a dog whose owner was close by with a leash in hand, telling him what he could and could not do. That was what Pierre did. He barked orders at Thor, and Thor obeyed—at least to a point.

Most of all, he hated the way the master watched him, with desire pouring off him in waves. As he thought about the number of "pets" the master took to bed with him, he cringed.

Not happening.

Not ever happening.

He swung his legs around on the bed and sat up on the edge of the mattress, the room around him pitch black. He balled the dark gray silk sheets in his hands. The master thought he treated his pets well because he gave them the "finer things," but sheets with a high thread count couldn't make up for all the horrors he made them commit.

Thor bent his head, doing his best to come to terms with what was happening to him. Since his return from Seattle, and his scrimmage with Walter Helmuth —a dick with a power complex who'd ended up being a gargoyle—Thor had been left with more questions than answers.

The dreams had begun to occur nightly after

that as well. Try as he might, he could not recall anything from the dream other than the name Lance. It was evident the name held deep meaning for him, but he was lost to what that meaning was. The name beat at him from within, demanding he acknowledge it.

What did it mean?

Who was Lance?

Was he tied to the past Thor could no longer remember? And why had the name been said to him more than once as of late while he was on assignments for the master? Could it be that Thor's name truly was Lance? If so, why couldn't he remember as much? Who was he before his rebirth as a vampire-shifter hybrid, as one of the master's playthings? Was he some kind of super soldier? A fucking ninja? And why were his memories of his life before gone?

Questions burned a hole in his gut and made him feel nauseous. Blackness was all that greeted him when he tried to remember a time before he'd come to be with Pierre. He knew he wasn't born a fully grown adult male, but it certainly felt as if he were. Since he'd woken to find the master above him, the man's lips stained red and his wrist bit open, Thor had known nothing else. Anything before his siring day was blank, and if anyone knew more details of his past, they weren't talking.

The little bit they had told him was that the Immortal Ops and the PSI-Ops were the enemy. He had been told the sole purpose of the other operatives was to kill supernaturals so that humans could rule the world.

The master's dislike of humans was well known, and many under him shared his opinion. Thor found he did not. Nor did he hate all supernaturals, as the master claimed the other operatives did. The master had plans for a superior race of supernaturals that would one day soon rule the humans, rather than hide in the shadows as they were forced to do now. Their numbers, while high, were no match for the humans, who bred at an exponential rate.

Pierre had been clear in his orders: Kill operatives whenever the opportunity arose, and kill as many humans as they wished without drawing attention to themselves.

So far, Thor had followed neither directive. He'd only followed Pierre's commands when he was dispatched to eliminate one of Pierre's hybrids who got out of control or who was drawing too much attention to their goal.

Such had been the case with Belial. Thor had developed a soft spot for the young supernatural, who had also been one of the master's pets. The man had also been a shifter before he was sired, so he could change into an animal and had a blood-lust. The same as Thor. But Belial had relished in the dark gift the master had given to them —vampirism.

Thor had not.

Belial had taken the dark gift too far. He'd slaughtered humans in a way and at a rate that had drawn too much attention to them all. And in the end, Belial had been nothing more than a pawn in Pierre's twisted game of life. He'd been used to root out a female Pierre had interest in. The woman had ended up being Belial's sister, but that didn't matter to the young supernatural. He'd tried to kill her all the same.

As Thor suspected had been Pierre's goal the entire time.

The master loved to play with people's minds and their lives. The pleasure Pierre got from his manipulations was sickening. And more and more, Thor had become aware of it all. Aware that everything was only a game to the master vampire. And while he was currently in the master's favor, that could change on a dime.

Thor had started to question everything he'd been led to believe. Seattle had been his breaking point. He'd been loaned out to Helmuth, who had been in charge of the Seattle paranormal under-ground scene. Helmuth orchestrated fight clubs that held death matches between supernaturals that he'd captured and forced to compete. Pierre had been fine with that behavior. It wasn't until Helmuth had partnered up with Gisbert Krauss that Pierre had taken note. Pierre had a working relationship with Krauss as well, getting many of his children from the mad scientist.

Krauss had taken to creating what could only be called berserkers for Helmuth. The berserkers were huge, way more powerful than the average super-natural male, and often looked like the stuff of nightmares. The one Thor had stood against while in Seattle was easily over seven feet tall and had about fifty eyes. A rocket launcher had taken it out, spreading creature goo everywhere in the process.

Whatever the creature had been prior to Krauss getting his hands on it was long gone. All that had remained was a monster.

From Thor's understanding, the creatures had been engineered to be sure bets against other super-naturals in the fighting rings for Helmuth. Guaranteed gladiators, who would bring in high-dollar clients to watch them slaughter others, but they'd been too hard to control, and had gone on killing rampages more than once in the city.

He pushed up from the bed and began to pace, feeling agitated as the past forced its way into his mind. It bubbled up inside of him like nervous energy, demanding he remember, as if some clue lie hidden within the horrors of his past. He balled his fists, tempted to beat his frustrations out on the wall until he was too exhausted to stand. Maybe then his mind would let him rest.

Thor had found himself fighting with an operative from the other side to battle the berserker, as well as botched hybrids that were under Helmuth's control. Thor had fought against Helmuth and his creations, knowing full well it might cost him his life should Pierre learn the truth.

Thankfully, Pierre's mistrust of the men he aligned himself with had played to Thor's advantage. It meant Pierre was quick to buy the lies Thor had spun. And spun he had upon his return. He'd told him partial truths, that Helmuth had been a gargoyle and had gone insane, and that Helmuth had unleashed the berserker on Thor. Wisely, Thor left out the bit about helping operatives from the other side.

Thankfully, the master had believed him. Helmuth was still a wanted man, and should he cross paths with any of Pierre's associates, he'd more than likely be killed on sight.

More than once, Thor had helped those whom Pierre labeled the enemy. The operatives Pierre seemed to detest continued to surprise Thor. Though he'd been told that whenever his mission overlapped one of the other operatives, he was to take the kill if presented, that had not been what happened. Each time he'd found himself near an Immortal Op (I-Op) or a Paranormal Security & Intelligence Operative (PSI-Op), Thor had ended up aiding in their mission and disregarding his own.

He didn't know why, but their fight and their cause resonated with Thor far more than his master's did.

Follow the master's orders without question.

Yet it seemed impossible. He was constantly at war with himself. His shifter side wanting to kill the master. His vampire side wanting to obey to a point. And the side that was just a man was lost in the inner struggle.

All he knew for certain was that he was funda-mentally broken. His will to serve the master was all but gone. Each day he had to remind himself who he served, and that the others were, in fact, the enemy.

Still, nothing seemed to satisfy his growing hunger to kill his master.

To bite the hand that had given him life was foolish and unheard of. He should have been filled with gratitude for the master vampire. Yet, each time Thor found himself near Pierre, he had to restrain his inner beast to keep it from lashing out at the man.

Thor was considered special to the master. A prized pet. Though he found himself with competition as of late. A newly sired hybrid had joined the mix in the last month, and Pierre had shown great interest in the man.

Pierre had given the man the name of Beowulf, and had started to watch the newcomer with the same intensity he did Thor. Desire emanated from the master whenever Thor was in his presence and, before the arrival of Beowulf, Thor hadn't noticed Pierre doing it to any of his other pets.

A little piece of him was thankful that Pierre's attention was being pulled in the direction of Beowulf, the shiny new toy. It meant a small reprieve from the master's lust-filled looks. Yet another part of Thor felt bad for the newcomer. Being the center of Pierre's attention wasn't fun.

Thor would know. He'd been in the position for just over a year, if his count was right. The first few weeks after his rebirth had been fuzzy and blended together. No one had given him hard timelines, so he wasn't sure how long he'd actually spent under Pierre's thumb to start with. It was beginning to feel like forever.

He took a deep breath, stretching his sore muscles. The dream had taken its toll on his body. His chest still ached. He rubbed it once more and walked to the bathroom off his bedroom. His sleeping quarters were extremely nice. As with everything involving Pierre, no expense had been spared.

Once in the bathroom, Thor flipped on the light, even though it wasn't needed. The bathroom was done all in calacatta marble. There were double sinks and a separate toilet room. The walk-in shower was so big that several people could have fit in it—not that he'd ever tried. Thor had never used the large soaking tub either.

He looked at his reflection in the giant mirror and noticed blood dripping from his nose. That was happening more and more too. It used to be accompanied by head-splitting pain. He wiped the blood away with the back of his hand, his focus going to his chest. There were no marks there. Nothing to indicate a source of the pain, yet it was there.

Phantom pain, he thought, running his fingers over his smooth skin. The faint smell of gunfire filtered over him again. Was that a phantom smell to go along with the pain? Was he remembering something?

Thor turned the water on and bent, cupping his hands in the sink. Cool water filled his hands, and he splashed it on his face, chasing away the blood and some of the unease he'd woken with. He remained like that for several minutes, continuing to splash his face with water.

He went to the giant walk-in shower and turned the water on, letting it heat. Once the bathroom had filled with steam, Thor slid off his silk pajama bottoms and stepped into the hot stream of water, letting it sluice over his body. He took the bar of vanilla-scented soap and rubbed it in his hands, building it to a lather. He ignored the smell of the soap, associating it with Pierre. He then began to wash, the hot water helping to loosen his sore muscles and chase away the phantom pains in his chest.

As Thor's hands slid lower, he found his cock hardening under the weight of his touch. While the opportunity to have sex was offered to him nearly nightly, he had yet to act upon it. Pierre's other pets seemed to relish offering blood and sex to one another—the master included. The idea of being with any of them sickened Thor.

He'd see to his own needs.

He closed his long fingers around the girth of his cock and turned away from the showerhead, stroking his shaft with the built lather. Closing his eyes, he let his mind wander to what turned him on. Instantly, he conjured a mental image of a tanned woman with olive undertones to her skin. His focus was her legs to start. She was tiny compared to him, and he liked that. It turned on his alpha side, knowing he'd be her protector as well as her lover. It didn't matter that she was merely a figment of his imagination. For now, she was real.

He pumped his hard, long cock, his mind still drawing images of his ideal woman. He could clearly make out the juncture of her thighs. Dark hair was neatly maintained on her mound, as if marking her sweet spot for him. Not that he'd need a map or anything. Deep down, he knew he could more than please a woman.

"Pfft, you used to be a total ladies' man," he said, gasping as he realized he'd remembered something of his past. It wasn't much, but he'd take it.

As he continued to work the lather over his cock, he tipped his head back, letting the water from the showerhead run over his shoulders and down the front of his body.

He thought of his imaginary woman's breasts. They were on the small side. He didn't like over-done ones. He liked them pert and sized just right. As he thought about what her face would look like, he found himself pumping his cock harder and faster. Full lips, a dimpled chin on a heart-shaped face. Large brown eyes, rimmed with thick black lashes. And a head of long, thick, wavy dark brown hair that fell over her shoulders.

"Ah, yes," he bit out as his ball sac tightened a second before his cock jerked. Seed erupted from him and was washed down the drain quickly, taking the evidence of his arousal with it.

Thor expelled a slow, shaky breath, an image of the perfect woman fading fast from his mind. The harsh reality of his existence came over him, reminding him that he was due in the main gathering room soon. He was charged with overseeing the others and keeping them in line. Pierre's safety was also a task allotted to Thor, though he felt like he might be the biggest risk to the master.

He finished showering then shut off the water and stood there for a moment, needing to draw on his willpower to keep up the façade that he was still one of Pierre's adoring minions. It was getting harder and harder to pull off. Soon he'd be discovered.

He was sure of it.

He'd gone too long between the feedings that kept his strength at full force, and it had been far too long since he'd last drank from the master. His lip curled at the idea of ingesting Pierre's blood. It had never tasted right to him. There was always a taint to it he couldn't explain and didn't want to dwell on. All he knew for sure was that without Pierre's blood, he'd eventually die. The master had been clear on that. Clear on the fact he was the giver and could be the taker of life.

Ingesting the master's blood was something most

of the pets did daily in some manner. Some drank straight from the source and others opted to drink from the bagged supplies of blood that held at least a few drops of Pierre's blood. Very few bags were untouched by the master's blood.

And those were the bags of blood that Thor gravitated toward.

There was part of the problem.

"I'm not feeding directly from him either," said Thor softly, knowing the walls often had ears. Secrets were hard to keep and even harder to live with. Betrayal was almost a given among the pets.

He toweled off and then headed back into the bedroom. Thor went to his wardrobe and surveyed his clothing options. As one of the master's favorites, he was provided with anything he wanted or needed. That included money and credit cards. It also included items he had no wish for; such was the case with the black leather skinny pants and black mesh shirt that had been on his bed the night prior.

Pierre liked to dress his pets in clothing he found attractive. Thor hated it. He was not a child's plaything to be dressed and led around. He was a man, and he had no intention of wearing the leather outfit.

More and more, he was taking a stand where he could. He'd stopped shaving his face daily, choosing instead to let a close-cut, sandy-blond beard grow in. His beard had flecks of white blond in it, matching his hair.

The acts of defiance were small, but they were all he had, and they helped him cope with his daily reality.

He selected a pair of dark gray, distressed, relaxed-fit jeans and a blood-red pullover cotton T-shirt that fit him snugly. For the last bit, Thor put on the black combat boots he'd bought while in Seattle. They were a sore point between him and the master.

A knock came on his bedroom door and he tensed. It was rare for anyone to bother him when he was in his room. He sniffed the air and caught the scent of wolf mixed with vampire.

Beowulf.

Chapter Two

THE URGE to snarl was great as the scent of a man Thor was fast starting to loathe came over him. Opening the door, Thor stood there staring at the man who matched him in height and build. Both stood well over six feet. Beowulf was no slouch in the muscle department either. Already Thor had sparred with him more than once. While he'd managed to best him, it had been a close call each time.

There was a wildness to the black-haired man. The kind of vibe that said Beowulf had no fear of death, no fear of pain. Beowulf's blue gaze always held a level of crazy that was normally reserved for the most broken of Pierre's pets. It was simply the man's everyday look.

Thor often wondered if he too was showing outward signs of insanity. "What do you want?"

Beowulf folded his arms over his leather-vest-covered chest. Leather bands circled his wrists, and he wore matching black leather pants. It was clear the master had selected his clothes as well. Though Beowulf didn't seem to have an issue with them, which surprised Thor. "You're a dick."

Thor prepared for a possible attack. "Came all the way up here to tell me that? How sweet of you."

"Yep. Dick," said Beowulf, clearly sizing Thor up for a rematch.

He stepped back from the doorway. "You seem really focused on my dick. Something I should know?"

Beowulf's gaze darkened. "No."

"Good to know. With what you're wearing, I was getting worried."

Beowulf snorted. "I didn't care enough about the outfit to put up a fight over it. And I didn't come up here to fight either."

"Could have fooled me," said Thor as he considered taking the first punch. "I generally assume anyone calling me a dick doesn't have my best interests at heart."

Beowulf shrugged. "I don't like you. That isn't really a state secret or anything."

"Feeling is mutual." Their last sparring match

had left both men nursing wounds. That was telling, as they weren't exactly easy to hurt as hybrids.

The other man rubbed his jaw, grinning slightly. The guy was seriously disturbed. "Master wants a word with you."

"He's risen already?" asked Thor, surprised that he hadn't sensed as much. It meant his bond to Pierre was weakening more and more with each passing day.

Beowulf lifted a dark brow. He jutted out his chin, his beard closely cut. His long hair was down tonight, falling to mid-back. He had a cover-model-meets-biker vibe to him that seemed to greatly appeal to Pierre. Versus Thor's Nordic godlike appearance, as the master had so often referred to it. "You didn't sense him wake?"

Shit.

Thor cleared his throat and shook his head. There was no point in lying so he went with a truth that could help explain it away. "I've not fed in days."

Beowulf continued to watch him. For a moment, Thor wondered if the man had changed his mind about coming up to start a fight. It wouldn't have shocked him. Beowulf had a short fuse.

"How is it you resist the pull of blood?" asked

Beowulf, his demeanor moving from threatening to curious in a matter of seconds.

The topic had come up more than once in Thor's time under Pierre's thumb. With every new batch of hybrids brought on, there was always one who wanted to know Thor's secrets to waiting so long between blood feedings. While he didn't like Beowulf, he hated the idea of being forced to live off blood more. From the genuine expression on Beowulf's face, he wasn't a big fan of having to answer to the bloodlust either.

With a sigh, Thor told him the truth. "I have discipline. I channel the need into the task at hand or working out."

"Why not just feed?" asked Beowulf, something off in his voice.

Thor had seen the man's repulsion at the fact they required blood to survive. It had been fleeting but there during Beowulf's conversion period. Because of the man's brute strength, Thor had been brought in early in the process to help control him. It was the first time Thor had been privy to the conversion process. He didn't remember his own, but he did know that he'd been out of commission for a long period of time during it all. The little bits he'd pieced together of the time weren't pretty. It had been painful and horrifying. An honest-to-God rebirth.

During Beowulf's conversion, he'd been taken off bagged blood and a woman had been brought in. She was so deeply mesmerized by Pierre that she hadn't had any real clue of the danger she'd been in.

Thor knew. He'd understood she wouldn't walk away from the ordeal. He'd been outnumbered, and he also knew if he dared try to save the human woman, he'd have been killed or worse—taken to Pierre's dungeons. Alive, he could try to right some of the master's wrongs; dead, he was of no help to anyone. He had to pick and choose his battles.

Beowulf had done his best to resist the urge to feed from the woman. Pierre had cut her throat enough to entice the newly turned hybrid, but not enough to let the woman die quickly. She'd bled out slowly, Beowulf there, smelling the blood, a hunger gnawing at him that no one other than a newly sired vampire could understand.

Thor had been shocked at the man's restraint, but he knew it would be short-lived. And it had been. The memory of it all still haunted Thor. He also knew deep down that something similar had more than likely been done while he was converting. And clearly, he'd done as Beowulf had—he'd surrendered to the bloodlust and lived to see another day.

Live to fight another day.

Pierre had missed the look of repulsion Beowulf had held that night, and Thor had filed the knowledge away, hoping to one day find an ally in the newcomer, not an enemy. Time would tell which way the coin would fall. For now, they still held a good deal of contempt for one another.

Beowulf lowered his gaze. "I need to know how you resist the urge to feed. I need a real answer."

"I'm sure you have already been told as much, but I didn't take to the dark gift as well as others," said Thor, hoping that, by pointing out what Pierre saw as a shortcoming, he could throw Beowulf off. It was the truth, he'd never developed the dark thirst to the extent of the others, nor had he developed their drive to kill everything around them.

Beowulf let out a long breath. "I understand."

There was a sadness in his voice that Thor understood all too well. It was all too easy to feel hopeless. "After I speak with the master, I can work with you in the training room, if you want."

"Will it help curb the hunger?" asked Beowulf, tipping his head, his fangs distending. He shook his head, his teeth returning to normal. "It eats at me from within. It's all I think about."

"I know," returned Thor, stepping closer to the man. He put a hand on Beowulf's shoulder. "Work with me in the training room tonight. It will help. Learn to channel it into something else, be it working out, or hell, even rage. You've got a lot of that built up. Use it to resist the need to feed daily. I've seen you eating real food. That means you didn't fully convert either. We just have to train your body to respond differently to the bloodlust."

Beowulf glanced away, shame evident on his face. "Pierre encourages me to feed as much as I want."

Thor knew that Beowulf could be playing him —gathering intel for Pierre on whether Thor was loyal—but that didn't stop him from speaking the truth. "He encourages a lot of things that aren't exactly on the level. I guess you have to figure out what your end goal is. Be like him, or not? I'm not a big fucking fan of being an indentured slave to the bloodlust—or to him."

"If he heard you say that, he'd punish you," said Beowulf.

Thor nodded. "Yep. Or find me amusing. Depends on the mood he's in at the moment."

"True. He's a fickle son of a bitch, isn't he?"

Thor didn't respond.

Beowulf swallowed hard. "What about resisting his blood? How is it you've gone so long without drinking from him?"

"First, you need to learn to control the bloodlust. From there, you work on controlling the urge to drink from Pierre."

"I hunger for a taste of his blood all the fucking time," Beowulf said, sounding disgusted. "And I don't even like the taste of his blood. It tastes off. Like old milk or something. Why the hell do I want it so bad? Is it because he's right? We'll die without his blood?"

Thor wasn't sure how to respond because he didn't have a good answer for the man. Hell, he'd had the same questions for as long as he could remember. Offering clarity on the subject wasn't something he could do. "I don't honestly know."

Beowulf nodded. "You're a dick, but you're honest. I respect that. I'll work with you in the training room when you're done meeting with the master."

Thor held his ground.

Beowulf gave a curt nod and then pulled away quickly. He walked ahead of Thor, down the long corridor, past the other doors, each a room for another of Pierre's pets.

Pierre's bedchamber was in the basement. He had a fear of light finding its way to him during the day. It didn't seem to matter that the windows were UV protected, and some rooms had the windows bricked over.

Pierre's paranoia knew no bounds.

Some of it was probably warranted. If his business associates were anything like him, they too were scheming to kill him and take what he had.

Thor made his way downstairs to the main living level and Beowulf splintered off, heading in the direction of the kitchen. Thor had a pretty good idea of what Beowulf was going for—the bagged blood stores they kept on hand. Thor would need to dip into the reserve soon if he didn't give in and feed. Even sucking on bagged blood made him hate the vampire side of himself.

Still, it was better than feeding from a human.

He really hated that.

It went against every fiber of his being.

The sound of music filtered through the air, and he cringed when he heard what was playing. Classical. That meant the master had not only risen for the night but was partaking in the nightly festivities. It would also mean there would be a high volume of blood and sex coming into play.

Thor entered the oversized room that held multiple antique, ornate loveseats and fainting sofas. All were upholstered in black material. Red accents filled the room and the walls were draped in blood-red fabrics. End tables were placed next to each sofa. The tables had white candles on them, each lit, offering the only light in the giant room. The room confused one's senses and made the occupants feel as if they'd stepped back in time, as everything in it was antique in some manner.

"Thor, come."

Thor tensed as the sound of his master's voice filtered over the large room to him. The Louisiana mansion wasn't one they normally spent a large amount of time in, despite its stunning spaciousness. The master had decided he wanted to spend a couple of months there so he'd issued the orders to make it so. Thor had grown used to the whims of his master. Used to the man acting like a spoiled child more often than not.

Unsure how old, exactly, the master was, Thor simply observed in silence. Already he was too far up in the ranks of the servants, and he'd achieved it in a short period of time. It was best to avoid drawing unwanted attention to himself, so he went along with whatever flights of fancy Pierre had.

"Thor," the master repeated, his tone held a warning—disobey again and there will be consequences.

Quickly, Thor tried to mask the disgust he felt at the very sound of the man's voice. If Pierre knew the truth, the best Thor could hope for was death. Pierre was criminally insane. He derived great pleasure out of others' torment and misery. And he had a stupid love of naming all his pets something from mythology. The very sight of the man caused Thor's fingers to curl as he pictured himself wrapping his hand around the vampire's throat and squeezing the life from him.

Stop, he thought, knowing Pierre would figure out Thor was no longer under his thrall.

Pierre sat in the center of the enormous room, on an oversized chair draped in red clothes. The chair was made to look like a throne, playing into the master's power complex. The man wanted everyone to obey him, and he wanted to rule the world. Already he was scheming to betray the criminals he'd aligned himself with.

They were in Louisiana because a longtime business associate of Pierre's was based out of the area, and the master had decided it was time to make a play for the man's territory.

On each side of the master vampire was a manservant, dressed in black leather pants and dog collars. Nothing more. Their chests had been well oiled, to make them shine and draw attention to them. The sight did nothing for Thor.

Another manservant knelt before the vampire, stroking the man's leather-covered leg. Pierre wore a puffy white pirate shirt and a pair of knee-high, lace-up leather boots. Thor had to bite back a laugh. The man looked ridiculous.

He lifted an imperious brow, his gaze raking over Thor's attire. His lip curled. "Why do you insist on dressing like you're about to dispense petrol at a service station?"

Glancing down at himself, Thor shrugged. His clothing choice felt right. He had his hair pulled haphazardly in a messy bun, acutely aware of how much Pierre disliked the look.

It made Thor want to wear his hair like that all the time.

"Where are the leather pants I had sent to your room?" demanded Pierre, reaching out and petting one of his manservants.

Thor cringed for the man. The manservant's mind was no longer his own. From the moment Pierre had put the human under his thrall, he'd been nothing more than a puppet. A walking blood bank and sex toy.

Thor's fingers clenched into a fist, and the overwhelming urge to charge the vampire and rip his throat out struck him hard. He wanted to let his mouth shift shape into animal form before sinking his teeth deep into the man's pale throat. He wanted to be brutal and feral. He wanted to be sure the man could not heal the damage.

As suddenly as the thoughts came over him, they were gone.

The near outburst was happening more and more as of late. The first time Thor had fought the urge to try to kill Pierre, it had scared him. Now he was used to it. Used to his hate and loathing of the master.

Everyone else he surrounded himself with seemed to adore him. They remained swept up and enraptured by him and his power. They saw him as a thing of beauty, power, and authority. Thor saw him as a puppet master. A monster. One he wanted to rid the world of.

But why?

Pierre had saved him.

At least that was what Thor had been led to believe. He'd been told by the master himself that the government had betrayed him and left him for dead. That Pierre's bite and his blood had breathed life back into Thor's broken body. Now he wasn't sure what he believed. The vampire was a master of lies and deception. And Pierre took great joy in manipulating circumstances to suit his twisted desires.

"Thor, you try my patience," drawled Pierre slowly, still petting one of his manservants. "Have you fed tonight?"

"No, Master," said Thor, careful to avoid glaring at the man. Feeding held little appeal to him. He didn't want Pierre to know that food seemed to sustain him far better than blood. With that said, Thor did notice his strength starting to wane when he went too long between feedings. He didn't like biting anyone and drinking from them. He preferred to drink from a mug or direct from the bag whenever he could find an untainted one, which also seemed to drive Pierre mad. "I wasn't hungry."

"Pet, we have been over this topic before. It bores me. If you continue to push back, I will force your hand in the matter," warned Pierre. "You are the only one of my pets who does not jump at the chance to feed. Some I've had to put down from drinking far too much, but not you. Why is that?"

Thor winced, thinking about the number of his brothers and sisters, those who had also been sired by Pierre, he'd been forced to hunt and destroy. They'd all gone mad with bloodlust, killing humans at an alarming rate. Some were savages when they killed, others killed cleanly, but far too often for Pierre's liking. For as insane as the man was, he knew they had to keep a low profile from humans or risk being hunted to extinction.

Pierre told stories of times long ago when some vampires weren't as careful to hide themselves among the living. They ate freely and did as they wished openly. Humans had risen up against them, as had the supernatural community. While vague on the details, Pierre's message was clear. Be as ruthless as you wish, but do not leave any evidence for humans to discover.

"Thor, your expertise and skill set are required

in New Orleans. I've made arrangements for you. You'll be heading out within the hour."

"What is it you need me to do there?" asked Thor.

With the flick of his wrist, Pierre dismissed the manservants near him and sat up in the large chair. "Gérard has sat on his ass too long, collecting the spoils of the territory. He lacks the drive he once had and is no longer fit to be a master with his own den. From what my spies tell me, Gérard's favorite pet is currently calling New Orleans home. Seek out Chilton. Discover why Gérard has him stationed there when he normally never leaves Gérard's side. Once you have that information, destroy him." Pierre glanced away and looked far off in thought before focusing on Thor, his gaze narrowing. "Make it messy. I want Gérard to get the message loud and clear. I am the new master here."

"Yes, sire," he said before turning to seek out Beowulf to inform him their training session would have to wait.

As suspected, Thor found Beowulf in the kitchen, sitting at the table, drinking from a bag of blood. He glanced up at Thor and pulled the bag from his mouth, his teeth coated in red. "Is he sending you to New Orleans?"

"You overheard?" That was impressive. Most newly sired hybrids didn't have that much control over their senses at first. That came with time and practice.

Nodding, Beowulf took another sip from the bag of blood. "Guess our training will have to wait."

Thor took pity on the man and grabbed a bag of blood for himself. He bit the top open and took a drink. While the liquid tasted great to him, the very idea of what he was doing sickened him. But he didn't have a choice. He'd gone too long without it and needed to build his strength, especially if he was about to go hunting.

Beowulf snorted. "My wolf isn't repulsed by blood either. It wants to hunt and kill prey though. It doesn't like the bagged shit."

Thor chuckled. "I get it. My panther isn't a big fan of it either. It likes the idea of killing for blood too, but I think it hates sharing me with the vampire side, so it behaves."

"Ditto," said Beowulf. He leaned back in the wooden chair. "I heard Pierre talking on the phone with someone before he sent me to retrieve you. Whatever's in New Orleans is pretty badass. Sounds like it has taken out more than one person sent to handle it. And I think we both know that while Chilton is a force to be reckoned with, he's not the ultimate evil that I'm hearing whispers of."

Thor remained in place, the bag of blood in his hand. "So, I'm being sent on a suicide mission?"

"Try not to be another notch in its bedpost. I like you more than most of these insufferable shitheads," said Beowulf.

Thor's brows met. "That's the nicest thing you've ever said to me."

"We're not gonna kiss or anything, so stop looking at me all doe-eyed," Beowulf grunted. "You're not my type. I'm not a fan of blonds."

Laughing, Thor headed out of the kitchen with his blood. "Asshole."

"Dick!" shouted Beowulf, only serving to make Thor laugh harder.

"There you go again, focusing on my dick!"

Chapter Three

EMANAIA (EMI) ZAHARIE looked at the couple near her and felt bad for the horrors they'd gone through. Their place was haunted by a malevolent spirit that had tried its best to not only run them off but ruin their relationship as well. They'd been terrorized in their safe haven, their home. Most would have already cut their losses and left, but the couple was stronger than that.

She admired that about them. Their strength had gotten them this far, and they were still standing. Not many would be after the ordeal they'd suffered. When most humans, with no past experience with the supernatural, came face to face with evil, they screamed and ran until they couldn't run anymore. Some even crawled under their covers, hoping that would keep the big bad monster from getting them. Spoiler alert. It never worked.

The couple before her had more gumption. More strength than most. When the horrors they'd been enduring escalated to physical violence, they went to a friend who, in turn, put them in contact with a local Catholic priest.

That was how Emi had come into the picture. Father Angelo was a friend of hers. When he'd done all he could, he'd sought her assistance.

Never having set out to be something of a ghostbuster, Emi had been reluctant to get involved, but when she'd heard what the couple had lived through, and then met them in person, she'd found it hard to say no. The desperation on their faces had moved her.

She knew what living in fear was like and wouldn't wish it on her worst enemy. It was why she'd agreed to come and do a house cleansing for them. She'd had no idea just how powerful the thing inhabiting their home would be. It had almost been too much for her, which was saying something, as she wasn't exactly a lightweight when it came to dealing with the dead or demonic. Yet this one had packed a lot of supernatural punch. Either her gifts were slipping, or she'd managed to uncover the one rock with a super spirit hiding under it.

"Is it over?" asked Helen Joy as she clung to her boyfriend. At twenty-five, they were both just starting their lives. They'd moved to New Orleans because they'd gotten jobs in the area and had romantic notions of what living in the city would be like.

They'd gotten far more than they'd bargained for.

Sam, the boyfriend, kept his arms around Helen Joy in a protective manner, his gaze darting around the small place. Everything was in complete disarray. The spirit had decided to flex its muscles and throw things about, causing Helen Joy and Sam to scream and shake in fear. Unimpressed with the theatrics, Emi had continued with her cleansing, ignoring items floating about and ducking when called for. That had only served to infuriate the spirit more. It had shouted threats and even appeared before Emi, though she'd been the only one able to see it.

The thing was ass-ugly. There was simply no other way to describe it. The spirit had drawn the short straw when it came to afterlife looks. It was locked in a state of rot mixed with the start of turning more monster-like than not. She'd seen that happen with bitter spirits. They stopped looking like the humans they'd once been and started looking like the stuff people told ghost stories about. It was as if their attitude became the defining factor for what they morphed into.

And the spirit in the house had a really bad attitude.

Surprisingly, she'd actually seen uglier ones. Some were so hideous they had lost any and all resemblance to a human. Then there were the ones that had never been human. Who had never had a soul. They were in the inhuman, or as most people called them, demons.

Demons pretty much sucked the big one. They were not only horrifying to look at, but they took malicious to the extreme. It was sport for them to ruin lives. Which was why she really friggin' hated demons.

Emi much preferred the formerly living to demons. She was used to the dead. Used to what they were capable of. That being said, the spirit she'd taken on this evening certainly had a lot of spunk and fire. Most of the dearly departed would have conceded by this point. Not the one haunting this building; it was determined to remain where it was.

It had teeth, and it wasn't afraid to show them.

Jerk.

Emi cast a warm look at the couple, who were

close to her age but seemed so much younger. Their eyes still held a certain innocence about them, despite what they'd been living with. They'd not seen as much as she had in their lives. This would be their traumatic life experience. A story they regaled others with at fancy dinner parties one day in the distant future. A footnote in the story of them.

This was nothing compared to what Emi had lived through. Simply thinking about her past again could take her back to that dark place. A place she couldn't go to mentally and come out on the other side whole.

She didn't want to scare Helen Joy or Sam, but she couldn't lie and tell them everything would be all right. It wouldn't. At least not yet anyway. There was still more to be done. "It's not gone. Father Angelo will be able to come back now and complete his exorcism. That will take care of it."

"It's still here?" asked Helen Joy, her voice shaking as she clung to Sam. Her blond hair looked wild from the ordeal. It had blown about and whipped into her eyes during the height of the spirit's tantrum. Prior to it all, she'd never looked anything but totally put together—wearing the latest in fashion, dressed in high-dollar clothes, her manners impeccable. But now she seemed lost, scared, disheveled.

Emi felt bad for her.

Helen Joy was a nice person with a good heart. She didn't deserve the fear and torment that the spirit had put her through. Not many did.

"Yes, it's still here," confessed Emi. "When Father Angelo came to me asking for help, I told him it would be a process. I was brought in to help weaken it to the point he could expel it. We've had to do something similar in the past more than once. It's worked well to date. I'm sure he cautioned you when he became involved that this wouldn't be fixed overnight. This spirit has been here a long time. It's powerful and angry."

Sam let out a shaky breath. Of the two of them, he'd been the one better equipped to handle the reality of their situation. From the get-go, he'd done his best to joke off the events, making light of them as much as he could. "And Rome wasn't built in a day."

"Right," said Emi. "The activity will calm for a while and it might seem like all is well and that he's gone. He's not. He's wounded right now, but trust me. He's still here. He'll strike back, and it will be worse than before. But you'll be ready for him. And Father Angelo is prepping for what he needs to do. When he comes back it will be with spiritual guns blazing."

The couple shared a look that said they didn't

think they'd be ready for anything, and were already pushed to their breaking point. She wouldn't be surprised if they decided to leave, giving up on their dream of living near the French Quarter or in New Orleans at all. She had to admit that if she were in their shoes, and had no real knowledge of the supernatural, she'd have wanted to run too.

"Remember what I told you," she said, hoping they'd listened when she'd explained everything in detail to them before starting the cleansing.

Sam nodded. "We need to show no fear, and we need to avoid challenging it."

Helen Joy touched his chin. "You can't provoke it anymore. Did you hear her?"

He sighed. "Yes. I'm sorry I challenged it. I didn't know it would lash out and hurt you to get back at me."

Emi could sympathize with their plight. She, more than most, understood that real evil was out there. She also knew they'd never survive if they tried to take on the dark energy headfirst. They simply weren't equipped to deal with it in such a way. "Yes, that's it. Wait for Father Angelo's call."

Helen Joy moved out of Sam's embrace and rushed Emi, wrapping her arms around her tight and hugging her. "Thank you," whispered the woman.

"It's not over," reminded Emi, returning the

embrace. She hated leaving them alone, but she couldn't stay. The cleansing had weakened her and she needed to be far from the house to regain her full strength.

"I know, but now we have hope."

Emi drew back slowly and took a long look at the couple. They loved one another. It was easy to tell. Their love was pure and true. It was the kind of love everyone deserved, but few received. They'd last no matter what. But they'd more than likely head out of town.

She couldn't blame them.

If she could outrun her problems, she would. Try as she might, she'd never been able to. At least not yet. She had a sinking feeling that the only way she'd escape her problems would be death. She wasn't willing to throw in the towel on life just yet.

I've got a lot of fight left in me too.

She gathered her bag and then headed toward the front door. Sam and Helen Joy would be all right at least for the next few days. By then, hopefully, Father Angelo would be able to rid the place of the bad entity. If not, Emi would go head to head with the spirit again; only this time she'd avoid holding back. In the end, it would learn she was the scarier of the two.

She left the couple to give the couple time

together by themselves. As Emi stepped out of the house, the heavy oppressiveness she'd felt inside lifted. Taking a deep breath, she savored the scents of the city she'd come to love.

When she'd arrived in New Orleans, she'd been a scared sixteen-year-old. She'd learned the lay of the land and who to avoid if you wanted to stay safe. She'd also built a network of friends of all ages.

Some were transients, like herself. Others had been born in the city and planned to one day die there. And some simply found themselves there, making a living doing what they loved.

Emi's Uncle Yanko had taught her how to use her skill set to make a living when she was young. He'd done much the same thing, as had her mother, whom she only knew from stories her uncle had told her. The siblings had been close, each possessing similar gifts. Her uncle would remark on how much Emi looked like her mother. She wouldn't know. There were no pictures of her parents that had survived the fire.

Emi had barely made it out of the flames alive.

Her uncle had saved her life when she was only three. He'd then raised her as his own, staying on the move with her, afraid to be in one place too long. The fear that whatever had killed her parents would come for her too had always been at the forefront of his mind. He'd done all he could to prepare her for the truth of what existed in the world—what went bump in the night. Bad things were real and quite capable of killing a person.

In the end, he'd paid the price for protecting her with his life.

Her heart hurt, thinking about Yanko. She missed him so much. Missed his laugh, the funny ways he'd tried to brighten her days. She even missed how serious he always got when training her. And mostly, she missed knowing she had a real family.

"You do have a family," she said softly, thinking of the people she'd come to know well in New Orleans—Hector, Nile, Cherry, and so many others. "They're just not related by blood."

She continued walking on the darkened side street, totally unafraid. She wasn't armed. She didn't need to be. She was a weapon all unto herself. Another gift her uncle had made sure to give her. And as much as she appreciated his training, she hated violence, doing her best to avoid conflict whenever possible.

She kept walking, finding as much joy and love for the buildings around her now as she had when she'd first arrived eight years ago. The homes on the street all sat on the edge of the sidewalk and had no front yards, as was the case with nearly every building on or near the French Quarter. She'd heard one of her friends who gave architectural tours to visitors describe the homes as cottages. They were all one story and had high-pitched roofs. They all had the same large windows that were shuttered over and the same two steps up to the entrances. Each was painted a different color. Some more vibrant than others.

That was something she loved about the city. People weren't afraid of color. And while the street should have felt cookie-cutter, as all the homes were the same style, it felt anything but. It screamed personality. Some people had planters filled to the brim with beautiful plants. Others had ferns hanging near their entranceways, and some had nothing. Yet they were all perfect to Emi.

Even the one with the evil spirit.

It wasn't the house's fault some jerk of a dead guy had decided to lay claim to it and scare anyone residing there.

Her feeling of euphoria died quickly as she felt the thrum of dark power pulsing over the area, as if searching for something or someone. It barreled at her in a way that was so fast and so powerful, she could almost see it. Pulling on what her uncle had taught her, she drew up her natural wards and froze in place a second before the ripple of dark energy blew past her.

She held her breath, as if that might help keep her from detection. It wasn't the first time she'd sensed the negative energy pushing out and over the city. It had happened nightly for the past several months. The first time she'd sensed it, she'd instantly been taken back to childhood, back to memories of flames surrounding her. Back to the horrors of losing her mother. While she could no longer remember her mother's face, she would never forget her screams.

Screams that had all been for Emi.

Emi shivered, the remembered pain bringing with it a chill. She hesitated, making sure the negative energy that had scanned the area was gone before she dared to move and pull a light sweater from her bag. Having lived in NOLA so long, she was always prepared for any type of weather, from a chill in the air to rain. It should have been too hot for a sweater, as it was still summer though on the latter end of it, but there was a nip in the air. One that only people sensitive to the other side and evil could feel. She knew the darkness searching the city was causing the chill, and she suspected she wasn't the only person feeling it.

A group of women staggered around the corner, each one holding the other up. She wasn't sure which was more intoxicated than the other. From all outward appearances, they were in a dead heat. When the redhead on the end tripped over her own two feet and nearly bit it face first, she won. The other two women with her cackled and helped her to stand upright—kind of.

The women spotted her and drew up short, still holding each other upright. The redhead smiled wide and laughed. "Ohmygod, look at her. She's dressed like a hippie chick."

The brunette next to her tried to shush the woman. It didn't work. The redhead continued making comments about Emi's choice of clothing.

Never one to care what others thought of her, Emi held her head high and kept walking.

"Wasn't she up by Jackson Square the other night telling fortunes?" asked a girl with a pixie haircut.

Hiccupping, the redhead swayed more and then laughed. "She looks like a Gypsy. You know, I heard they're all thieves."

The brunette tugged harder on the redhead. "Crystal, enough. That isn't true and it's not polite to call them Gypsies."

Emi hid her laugh. Her mother's people were Roma. Had her uncle still been alive, he'd have found humor in the women as well. He had never cared how others referred to his heritage. He had bigger things in life to worry about. Like real-life monsters.

Ignoring the women, Emi kept walking in the other direction. To her surprise, she felt the dark energy scanning the area again. It had never done it more than once in a night.

As she had before, she came to a grinding halt, drawing upon her natural wards, waiting for it to pass. It took its time, weaving in and out of every nook and cranny. When it reached her, she remained perfectly still, afraid to so much as breathe.

Again, memories of her childhood came flooding back. It took all she had to keep from shuddering and drawing attention to herself. The second the energy moved on, mystically searching other areas, she ran in the direction of her home. She didn't need it spelled out for her. The darkness was on the hunt, and when it found its prey, there would be more blood on the city's streets.

There had been an increase in murders in the months since its arrival, and she knew that wasn't a coincidence. Whatever the thing was, it was a killer. Plain and simple.

Deep down, she knew she should try to seek it out and destroy it, but there was a level of fear there that she'd not experienced since she was a child. Whatever it was, it was powerful, and the odds were it would wipe the floor with her. Still, innocent people were dying, and she might be able to stop it. The dilemma had eaten at her conscience for weeks.

For now, she needed to rest. She'd expended a great deal of energy helping Helen Joy and Sam.

Chapter Four

THE SLIGHTEST HINT of dawn began to show in the sky and relief started to sweep through her. The dark energy always vanished during the daytime.

She quickened her pace, making her way down the side streets, weaving back in the direction of the French Quarter. When she spotted a boarded-over building that at one point had been painted a shade of blue with hints of gray, she exhaled. Home sweet home. She made her way around to the side of the building and pulled open one of the loose pieces of particle board.

Emi walked through the rundown hallways of the building she'd taken to calling home. It had seen better days. Much better days. At one point it had been beautiful, as noted by the hidden architectural details throughout, but that time had been long ago.

At some point in its life span, it had fallen into disre-pair, and no one had taken the time or money to bring it back to its former glory. Its reputation preceded it and the owner had been unable to sell, so he'd permitted it to rot.

The saddest part was, it was still inhabited by spirits who did remember when it was beautiful. The ones who knew they were dead spoke of how it used to be, and the few who still didn't believe they'd crossed over saw it the way it was, not the state it was truly in.

Denial was a beautiful thing.

Still, she felt a strange bond with the home. Able to sense what had happened within its walls over its life, Emi felt pity for the building, wanting it to know peace and love within it once again. It had an ugly past, filled with murder, despair, and evil, but she was doing her part to dispel that and help it find its way back to peace. For all its horrors, it had been home to happiness as well. Of good times, parties, laughter, and even several weddings. It had seen children born and raised in it. Like a person, it had good and bad in its life.

A shadow shot past her so quickly that it made her long dark hair move. Emi reached up and adjusted the scarf she wore much like a headband. She ignored the entity, seeing it for what its brush-by was—an attempt to frighten her. It would take far more than shadow figures to send her packing. She'd seen real evil in her life. The darkness in the house didn't compare.

The door at the end of the hall opened and a young man in his mid-twenties stepped out. He always looked disheveled, but Emi knew that was what he was aiming for. It was part of his way to protest. Though she'd never been fully clear on what, exactly, he was protesting. He came from a good home, from a family who had means and were good to him. So good that they gave him a monthly stipend to live off of, but he chose instead to squat in the building with her and the spirits who called the abandoned place home.

"Hey, Emi," said Taylor, smiling wide.

She returned the smile and came to a stop, noticing he had a bag slung over one shoulder. "Are you going somewhere?"

"Home for a bit," he confessed, looking marginally embarrassed over the revelation. "My sister is having a baby, and I'd like to be there for her."

That was great news. Taylor had pulled away from his family somewhat, only touching base when Emi asked about them all. It was good to hear he'd reached out on his own and had the desire to be there for his sister, whom he spoke of often.

"I bet Colorado is beautiful this time of year," she said, having had long talks with him about his family before. They lived in Fort Collins, Colorado, and ran a tech firm that was located there. Taylor would talk about his time spent at Rocky Mountain National Park, and all the time he spent exploring the state. She'd never been there, but the mental picture he'd painted for her seemed wonderful.

Taylor had been given the finest in educations and had been expected to take over the business. Instead of doing that, he'd moved to New Orleans. He'd quickly fallen in with a group some of the locals took to calling gutter punks, though Emi didn't like the name.

She also didn't care much for the group Taylor had fallen in with. Thankfully, he'd been slowly breaking away from their toxic influences. He'd even reached out to her, asking if he could stay in the same building she'd been calling home for nearly a year. She'd warned him that it wasn't for the faint of heart, that it was haunted, and he'd been fine with it all. Of course, he'd not actually believed her to start with, but quickly learned she'd been telling the truth.

It had only taken one long night of the items in his room being tossed about by an angry entity for Taylor to see the light. As if that hadn't been enough, Fredrick had decided to show himself to Taylor once. It had been brief, but that was all that was needed. Taylor had screamed and run out of the house, refusing to enter again for hours. Emi explained that Fredrick was harmless and good-natured. Taylor hadn't looked like he believed her.

He glanced back at the door he'd come from then gave her a wary look.

She stepped closer. "Things still moving on their own in there at night?"

"Yeah. Around three in the morning," he said with a shudder. "I watched my books levitate for over an hour. Does the thing ever get tired?"

"That was just Mrs. Pumpernickel again," said Emi, nearly laughing. The spirit was one who didn't accept she was dead. She understood she was, but she didn't act like it. To her, it was just another day. Taylor's room was once hers, so she tended to move things around, scaring the daylights out of Taylor in the process. It was never her intent to do so. She never really seemed to notice Taylor, only Emi. And she didn't see the house for what it had become. To her, it was her crowning glory.

"I know you say she's a nice older woman, but she gives me the creeps," said Taylor, shuddering again. "Plus, what kind of name is Pumpernickel?"

Emi grinned. "She can't help her last name is the same as a kind of bread. She's a talker, but she's got a big heart."

Taylor glanced around. "Not everything here does."

She knew he was talking about the evil entity that lived there. He was right, that didn't have a good heart at all. "Never show it any fear."

"I don't know how you do it. You get the worst of it here, but you stay." He put his hand on her shoulder lightly. "Come with me to Colorado. I'll buy your ticket. We can find work out there and get away from all this. We can make a life for ourselves there."

Putting her hand over his, she sighed. Just as she suspected Helen Joy and Sam would do soon enough, Taylor had realized he'd reached his supernatural breaking point. "You've had enough of it all, haven't you?"

She wasn't just talking about the ghosts, those she knew those were a hot-button issue. Taylor had been having problems with the group he'd fallen into since coming to New Orleans—the gutter punks. They were a rough bunch of criminals. Sadly, he'd started to go that route as well, but had cleaned up his act. She could only hope he would decide to cut his hair and shave his face at some point too. Under all the scruffiness was a handsome man. She was sure of it.

"Yeah," he said with a sigh. "Austin is pissed with me. I refused to do magik tricks down on Royal, so he's got the whole crew looking for me. And I think he figured out I'm going home."

Emi could only imagine how mad Austin was. He was the head of the group Taylor had run with and fancied himself a gang leader in a lot of respects. He wasn't a good person. He'd beaten more than one person to the point they'd ended up in the hospital.

"Did he hurt you?" she asked, worried for Taylor. More than once, Austin had injured Taylor. Her friend wasn't a fighter.

He shook his head. "No, but only because he's scared to come in here after the last time."

She hid her smile. There were perks to living in a haunted house. The one and only time Austin had entered the house, he'd found himself instantly on the wrong side of Fredrick's patience. Fredrick had lived in the home since before New Orleans was even a city. He was well aware that he'd passed, and had no intentions of leaving. He would be forever earthbound if he got his way.

That was fine by her, she loved him dearly. He was protective of her and she appreciated it. He'd not taken kindly to Austin and his threats. By the time Fredrick was done pulling a full-on poltergeist, Austin was screaming and running down the street like a bear was chasing him.

The memory still made her laugh.

It had also been the only time Taylor had

laughed about the paranormal activity within the home.

Taylor closed his eyes. "Living this kind of life is not what I'd thought it would be."

"No. I expect not," she said, surprised it had taken him this long to realize he wasn't cut out for a life on the streets.

He had a choice.

She didn't.

If she tried to live a real life, there was a chance what killed her mother would find her. While she wasn't exactly sure what it was, she knew it was more than human. And she knew it had terrified her uncle, who didn't fear much.

No. She didn't get options.

She was alone in the world, and it was best she remain so. She'd taken a risk becoming close friends with people in the city. She knew better. Everyone around her always ended up hurt or dead. It was why she kept Taylor and the others she'd met since arriving in the city at a bit of an emotional distance. They knew some of what she was capable of, but they didn't know her backstory, and they never would. Not if she could help it. She wanted them safe. Bringing them into her world of darkness fully would lead nowhere good.

"Thank you for offering to take me with you, but here is where I'm supposed to be," she said softly. Though she had to admit that the idea of running away from it all was appealing. "At least for now. Who knows what tomorrow will bring?"

He squeezed her shoulder gently and his emotions ran over her, another curse of her gift. "You shouldn't be here in this place alone. It's not safe."

She nearly laughed. The haunted building that had a dark entity inhabiting it was far safer than what she'd faced in her life. "I'll be fine. I promise."

Taylor moved his backpack around to his front and unzipped it. He pulled out an envelope and handed it to her. When she opened it, her eyes widened. There had to be at least five thousand dollars there.

"Take that and find a safer place to live, Emi. Get on a train. A bus. A plane. Whatever. Go anywhere but here. You see dead people and are living in a city filled with dead people. There's something in this house that needs a team of priests to get it out, and you keep going out in the city and battling even scarier shit. You think I don't know about what you do out there, but I hear things. It's not safe for you. Come away with me."

She thrust the envelope back at him. "I can't accept that. Thank you, though."

He put his hands over hers, refusing to take the money back. "My parents send me this much and more each month. It's pocket change to them. Take it. I don't need it, but you do."

"Taylor," she stressed. While his gesture was incredibly kindhearted and generous, she didn't feel comfortable accepting the money.

"Emi," he returned, his gaze stern, saying he wouldn't waver. "You were there for me when I lost my way. Let me be here for you now."

She didn't want the money, but it was clear he wasn't going to take no for an answer. Emi eased the envelope from his hands and then hugged him, her five-foot-six-inch frame seeming small in comparison to his well over six-foot one. While he wasn't a fighter, he had the body of one. She suspected that came from all the skateboarding he did around the city.

Taylor's arms wrapped around her and he held her to him, longer than one should for a friendly embrace. She let him, knowing he'd worry about her while he was away. She hoped he found what he was looking for back home and decided to stay near his family. If she still had family left, she'd have moved heaven and earth to be near them.

"Send word through Hector when you get settled in out there," she said, stepping back and ending the hug. The urge to cry was there, but she resisted, knowing if she broke down, Taylor would never leave. He'd stay for her and, in the end,

Austin and his crew would hurt him, or Taylor would get wrapped up in drugs again and lose himself.

Taylor met her gaze then dug in his bag again before pulling out a cell phone. "Here. It's a prepaid one. I'll worry less with you having it."

She shook her head. "No. Thank you, but technology and I have a longstanding history of not getting along." It was the truth. She tried to avoid anything technology-wise as much as possible. For some reason, she tended to make watches stop, phones break without any sign as to why, and computers simply die on her. She never bothered owning a television or anything of worth because her body would somehow manage to short it out without warning or reason.

Driving a car seemed unwise, with all the issues she had with anything electronic. Besides, the city offered everything she needed to be mobile.

He snorted. "Come on, Emi. Take the phone. I'm not accepting no as an answer."

"Taylor, it's for the best if you just write to Hector," she stressed. He'd not been around when she'd made the small microwave he'd gotten them explode by simply standing too close to it for an extended period. To this day, he thought she'd put something metal in it by mistake. "He'll make sure I get your letters, and I can send you responses through the mail."

Bending, he kissed the tip of her nose. "You're adorable. You know that, right?"

She stepped back, wanting to avoid encouraging him more. She'd sensed his feelings for her had started to change over the months they'd known one another, but she'd hoped it would pass. That he'd see she only wanted friendship from him. Emi had never had any real interest in finding Mr. Right, or any man for that matter. She liked her life as it was, uncomplicated. Besides, who would want to be with a woman who spoke to the dead and vanquished evil spirits, not to mention spent most of her life being hunted by a boogieman?

She didn't think too many men would want that baggage. Taylor didn't know everything about her, and for good reason.

"Have a safe journey home," she said, looking up at him.

With a sigh, he eased past her in the hall and then paused. She used his moment of distraction to shove the envelope full of money back into his bag. She'd meant what she'd said. She couldn't accept it. She worked for everything she had.

He glanced over his shoulder at her. "Are you sure I can't entice you to join me? My parents have been at me for ages to bring home a nice girl."

With a snort, she pushed on his backpack. "Get going there, buddy. And trust me when I say your parents would not be happy if you brought home a girl who sees dead people and other people's pasts and futures."

He laughed. "Are you kidding? My mom is all into having her fortune read. I've already told her about you more than once, and that you read tarot cards. She's wanted to meet you for months. Plus, I think she sort of wants to thank you for getting me to see the light and come home."

"Get going," she said with a smile. "And stay out of trouble."

"Will you look after Rocky for me?" he asked, a note of sorrow in his voice.

Rocky, the stray dog that Taylor had sort of adopted, tended to come and go from the building as it pleased. He was a sweet mutt that was a mix of too many types of dogs to ever be able to identify its breed.

"Of course. That goes without saying."

Taylor teared up, but headed for the end of the hall all the same.

Chapter Five

EMI HURRIED in the direction of the staircase that led to the upper level of the old home. She didn't dare look back, already feeling Taylor's gaze on her, heating her as she walked. He needed to go to Colorado and get far from the city. There was something dark in town that scared her far more than the entity in the house, more than the thing haunting Helen Joy and Sam.

The less-than-pleasant entity in Emi's home liked to toss things around and tug at her hair while whispering threats. Whatever was in the city, hunting, was far more dangerous. It had killed more than once, and it wouldn't stop until someone destroyed it.

"That someone might have to be you," she whispered to herself.

She made it to the top of the stairs and walked wide, to the left. The floor was weak in the center. Fredrick, her favorite of the spirits haunting the home, said it was dry rot, and had wanted her to ask Taylor to fix it. Taylor wasn't really handy so she'd never bothered.

"He has feelings for you."

Emi kept walking, smiling as she heard the voice of someone she considered a friend. She didn't bother turning around. She knew nothing would be there. Fredrick only showed himself to her when he felt like it. The fact he was living-challenged didn't stop him from weighing in on her personal life whenever he got the chance. He had an opinion on everything and always had her best interests at heart.

He'd become something like family to her, and she appreciated him knowing she didn't quite want to be alone just yet. It hurt that Taylor was leaving, but it truly was for the best. Nothing good would come from him remaining in the city. He needed to be home and with his family.

"He *thinks* he has feelings for me," she corrected as she walked down the hall in the direction of the room she'd claimed for herself.

"If you say so," said Fredrick with a soft chuckle. There was a grandfather quality about him that had always appealed to her. She'd never known any of her grandparents, and her uncle had always teared up when she asked—so she'd stopped asking.

She knew he was close at her heels even though he wasn't showing himself. She could feel his presence. The smell of tobacco mixed with oranges always accompanied his arrival.

She exhaled slowly, knowing Fredrick was right. "Taylor and I aren't meant to be together. It would never work."

"Because he's human and you're not?" asked Fredrick.

In life, he'd been like her, more than human. He was tight-lipped on just how much more, but she knew he was something. She cringed. "Yes, and there is the fact I don't see him in the same light. He's my friend. Nothing more."

"I know that. Sad that he doesn't seem to let it soak in fully," said Fredrick.

Emi nodded. "I need to rest and then get ready to do some readings tonight."

"You're not planning to go to the square, are you?" demanded Fredrick as she entered her room. "That darkness is still out there and the French Quarter has become its favorite hunting grounds. You will deny it, but I think it's hunting you."

So did she, but admitting it out loud wasn't something she could do. It would only cause Fredrick to worry more. He'd been dead long enough to have a good deal of power, plus, the fact he'd been more than human while alive only added to it. He could make it difficult for her to leave the house if he wanted to. And he would if he thought he was protecting her.

She loved him for that. "Thank you for your concern, but I'm okay. I promise. And I have to work."

"You could just guess the lotto numbers," he said, only half joking.

"What do you know about the lotto?"

He snorted. "People who have lived here over the years have had televisions and radios. I learn things."

She laughed. "Look at you, you man of the world."

He chuckled as well, and then the feel of him grew stronger. "Maybe take tonight off. Stay in. Something feels off out there."

"I'll think about it. For now, I want a bath and then rest," she said, turning around in the room near the bed.

The old iron bed frame had been left behind sometime over the years. Its size was part of the issue, as was the fact that it tended to shake on its own—which had more to do with spirits than it did the frame itself. Anyway, it had come to remain in the home and had ended up hers. It had a newer mattress that Hector and Taylor had helped her carry in a few months back. Before that, she'd slept on the worn old one. It hadn't been pretty or smelled great, but it had been a place to lay her head out of the weather.

More than once she'd not been provided that luxury, and she knew better than to look a gift horse in the mouth.

The room was sparsely furnished, but she didn't have much, so it was perfect for her. In one corner was a folding table and two chairs that she often took to Jackson Square to read tarot cards for tourists. She had two different cloths she used as table coverings, alternating between them as the mood struck. One was a deep, shiny purple and the other was a matte black. To the side of the table and chairs was a clothing rod on wheels.

Taylor had found it for her when someone had put it out for trash pick-up. He'd brought it back to the house and hung up her clothing for her. She'd been touched by the gesture, as it had been the first time in years that she'd felt somewhat moved into a location. Normally she simply lived out of a duffle bag. She didn't have much in the way of clothing, but what she did have suited her personality. She liked long, flowing skirts, tank tops, sweaters, and scarves.

To the far right of the room lay a black velvet

bag. In it was her deck of tarot cards that had been passed down to her from her uncle. Next to it was a bag that was similar in size but held various crystals. She looked at the small shelving unit near them and sighed. Her herbs, crystals, and candles were all out of order.

"The demon was up to no good again," said Fredrick, sounding tired. He and a few other spirits in the house had started to take a stand against the evil that had taken up residence there. Prior to Emi's arrival, all the spirits had lived in fear of the dark entity. Not anymore—and it was losing strength because of it.

"Jerk," she said to it, knowing it was listening. "I'm going to shove a white candle up its backside if it keeps messing up my shelf."

Fredrick laughed and then showed himself. He wore clothing indicative of the time he'd lived. In his late fifties, he'd lived a long life for his time. He'd been murdered in the house and there ever since. Though she'd offered to help him move on, he'd elected to stay and watch over the other spirits that remained. He had taken on a fatherly role to everyone, including her. In some ways, his protective energy reminded her of her uncle, whom she missed terribly.

Emi went to the window and looked out at the rising sun. With the sunrise came a reprieve from the feeling that whatever darkness was in the city was looking for her. She'd learned early on that it didn't prowl the streets of NOLA during the daylight hours.

Her uncle had explained creatures like the one who made the dark energy to her when she was little, making sure she was prepared for what life would bring. He had told her tales of her family's legacy, of their history, and how they'd always walked parallel to the creatures of the night. How they were a counterbalance of sorts. She'd always thought his tales to be silly stories. Something he'd invented to help explain away her parents' deaths when she was still too little to remember them passing. It wasn't until she'd seen the truth of it all with her own eyes that she knew her uncle hadn't been telling tall tales.

He'd been preparing her for life.

A lone tear escaped her as she thought of her uncle. Yanko had died at the hands of a monster and, from that point forward, she'd been on her own, making a go of it. Now, at twenty-four, she wondered if this would always be the way of it. Would she always live off the grid, barely getting by, letting only a few people into her inner circle?

As she stared out at the rising sun, she heard the water in the bathroom tub come on. She never questioned how it was Taylor had managed to get running water to the building when it was clear that it had been without for so long. She did know that Taylor had rigged up a system that left them borrowing power from the strip bar next door. She didn't harbor much guilt over it, even though she knew it was wrong.

She knew without looking that Fredrick was seeing to it she had a warm bath drawn. He liked to make sure she took care of herself.

"Did you rid the young couple's house of the evil entity?" he asked from the bathroom.

"No. It's been there a long time. It's strong. I wounded it," she said with a soft sigh. "When I left, I felt the darkness in the city again. It was strong. I think it killed last night. That was why I could feel it so much."

"The police will cover it up. They won't risk tourism falling because of a rising body count," said Fredrick from the bathroom. The sound of running water stopped. "Your bath is ready. I'll be downstairs if you need me."

"Thanks," she said, still staring out the window.

"Emi, I know you won't listen, but we all wish you'd stop drawing attention to yourself by using your gifts. Whatever is out there is hunting people like you—people with magik. It has the other side scared. Even the dark power that lives here is fearful of it."

"It's my duty to help protect those who can't protect themselves," she said, repeating the words her uncle had instilled in her from a young age. "The couple needed someone to step in. I couldn't leave them to fight it on their own."

"You could have told them to get out of the house," said Fredrick.

She nodded. "I could have, but the thing there would have just kept terrorizing everyone who moved in."

"It still will," said Fredrick.

"Not once Father Angelo is finished with it," she said.

Her uncle had been the one to teach her about spirits and how to deal with them. Both good and bad. Growing up with her uncle had been a unique experience, and she knew no different. She'd never had a real home. Every place she'd lived had been temporary, and rarely did they have running water and electricity. They had gotten by and continued the good fight—protecting humans from things they didn't even think were real.

Monsters.

Things that went bump in the night.

And some things that weren't hindered by sunlight.

It was all she'd ever known.

With a heavy heart, Emi headed into the bathroom. At one point in the home's past, it had been renovated, but time had not been kind. The claw-footed tub still held water but had permanent hard-water stains. The subway tiles on the wall were cracked in some spots and totally missing in others. The black-and-white-striped wallpaper above the tiles, partway up the wall, showed the aged, older paper beneath it. There was a huge water stain in the upper corner of the ceiling from where the roof leaked. The sink was broken on one edge but it still held water and functioned, so she thought it was perfect. The toilet worked, and since many of the places she'd called home in her life had been without a working one, she was pleased.

Her favorite part of the room was the huge mirror that hung on the wall. It was old and had a bit of water damage on one side, but it was still beautiful and ornate. She didn't understand why it had been left behind, but it didn't surprise her too much. With the number of spirits in the home, it stood to reason that occupants would vacate quickly out of fear, leaving behind things they normally wouldn't.

Emi took her red cami off and set it on the sink's edge before slipping off her long yellow and red, flowered, flowing skirt, doing the same with it as she had the top. She tied her hair into a loose bun on top of her head and then climbed into the tub.

When she felt the warm water on her body, she smiled and glanced in the direction of the bathroom door.

"Fredrick, you're an angel!" she yelled, knowing he'd tapped into his powers to warm the water for her. It was amazing what spirits who had been earthbound for a long time could do. With each passing year, they became more powerful. Such was the case with Fredrick.

Chapter Six

AUBERI BOUCHARD GRUNTED as his fellow Crimson-Ops teammate, Searc Macleod, turned on the lights in the hotel room. It was as if stadium lighting had been installed without Auberi's knowledge. For a minute, he worried Searc had decided to end it all and had let in sunlight—something they both did their best to avoid.

"Rise and shine, Frenchie," said the Scottish vampire, as he proceeded to go through the hotel room turning on every light he could find. When he began to hum a song from Scotland of old, Auberi considered getting up to kill his technically already dead friend. They'd known each other a long time and trusted one another without question.

"You know you're a dick, right?" asked Auberi.

"Aye," returned Searc, adding words to his song.

Shielding his eyes, Auberi snarled, his vampire eyes sensitive to the light. He'd gone out partying the night prior and didn't feel like he'd slept at all. He closed his eyes and felt around for his phone, knocking it from the bedside table as he did. He cursed again as he leaned to retrieve it, the bed sheets pulling low, exposing his nude body partially.

"For fuck's sake," snapped Searc, his brogue coming through even more than normal. "I do nae need to see yer naked self. Cover up."

"You're the one in *my* hotel room. And you're the one who helped himself in without knocking," Auberi said, finding his phone and pressing the button to check the time. He frowned as he saw it was well past sunset. He should have felt fully rested. He didn't. He felt a lot like he'd been hit by a bus. "What the hell did Blaise give me last night?"

"I do nae know, but you should know he looks far worse than you," said Searc from the window area.

Auberi had gone out with his teammate, Blaise Regnier, and a man he considered one of his best friends, Malik Nasser. All the men were technically PSI-Ops, but Malik wasn't a card-carrying member of the Crimson Sentinel Ops, also referred to as the Fang Gang by other operatives, because they were comprised fully of vampires. Malik was a lion-shifter, and could walk without issue in the sun's light. That was something most of the vampires in PSI struggled with.

Auberi missed the sun, to a point, but had learned to live his existence in its absence. He'd seen many of his brethren turn ugly with hate as the years ticked by, leaving them trapped in darkness. There were days he felt the pull to the side of evil, but he resisted. At least for now. Time would tell if he'd remain strong or if the lure of the demon he carried within him would win, as had been the case with more than one of his blood brothers.

You will not become Pierre, he thought, the idea of turning into what Pierre had become too much for Auberi to fathom.

Malik had been temporarily tasked to Auberi's Fang Gang unit as they continued to try to hunt for leads on The Corporation and its key players. That was what had led them to New Orleans. They'd been tracking a group of newly formed vampires who had partnered up with a large number of hybrids.

That had led to nothing good.

The death count in the city was on the rise, and those in the area who worked hard to hide the truth of supernaturals' existence from humans were running out of ways to cover up the crimes. Already the digital underground was linking the increase in crime and violence to supernaturals. It had been all the PSI tech teams could do to try to pull down the blogs and forums. They'd get one down, and four more would pop up, each talking about the truth of supernaturals, of PSI, of the Immortal Ops, of The Corporation. If the information managed to find its way to the mainstream media outlets or took root with everyday, non-crazy conspiracy theorists, it would lead to mass pandemonium.

Humans really liked to panic.

Morons.

"Yer lazy. Get up," stressed Searc, sounding like a mother hen. He used to be fun. Since he'd mated, only a week prior, he'd become boring. That had to be a record.

Auberi lay in bed, quivering at the thought of being tied to one person the rest of his immortally long life. As much as he longed for companionship, he didn't want it at the high price tag that came with a mate.

The loss of freedom.

No.

He much rather preferred the single life. He could come and go as he pleased, and party with his friends as often as he wanted. More importantly, he could bed who he wanted, when he wanted. He liked that freedom most of all, and couldn't imagine wanting only one person for always.

He shuddered again at the thought.

"I'm too old for New Orleans," said Auberi, feeling every century he had under his belt.

Searc hummed merrily as he continued to make his presence known in the most annoying ways. The man had been mated for a week, and already his eternal Susie Sunshine demeanor was becoming an issue. Auberi hated to say he missed the old Searc, but the always-smiling one was freaking him out. He liked to think he was open to just about anything. Eternal optimism wasn't on the list. "Go away, or I'll get out of this bed and do jumping jacks naked."

"Gah, do nae even think of it," said Searc, throwing a pair of slacks at Auberi. "Get dressed. We've bad guys to hunt."

"In a hurry to get back to your mate?" asked Auberi, already knowing the answer to the question. A mate was someone created specifically for a person's other half—their perfect someone. Searc had been lucky enough to find his mate, and he'd finally gotten around to claiming her. Now, the entire team was subjected to Pollyanna. It was part of why they'd decided to go out on the town and party their first night in.

Searc had wanted to video conference with his woman, and none of the men wanted to hang around the hotel while Searc and his mate, Jessie, made lovey-dovey noises at one another over the internet. Instead, the single men had taken off and done their best to party as if there was no tomorrow. Auberi wasn't sure how much alcohol they'd consumed, but he did know it was far more than humans could have withstood. And with the way he still felt, after having slept several hours, he could only imagine how far gone they'd all been.

He smacked his lips together. "Gah. Cottonmouth."

Searc pitched a water bottle in Auberi's direction and gave him a hard look. "Get dressed. The sun is down. We could already be on the trail of the bad guys."

The door to the room opened and Malik appeared, wearing a pair of sunglasses, looking like he wanted to rip Searc's head off.

Auberi remained in bed, the covers only just barely covering his groin. He wasn't one to sleep in clothes. "Let me guess, he came barging into your room, turning on all the lights too?"

Malik lowered his sunglasses, his gaze narrowing on Searc. "Will anyone miss him if I kill him?"

"His woman would," said Auberi, standing and putting his back to his friends. Cool air from the room moved over his exposed backside.

"Auberi, cover your French arse!" snapped Searc.

Auberi glanced over his shoulder at his backside and then grinned at Searc. "How about I turn around and show you my very French front side?"

Malik snorted and crossed his arms over his chest. "I had to get up and get dressed. You're not getting out of this either. I'll drag your naked ass out there to hunt these hybrid dickheads."

Auberi batted his eyes. "Say my naked ass again. Sexy."

Malik's jaw hardened. "I'll kill you too when I'm done killing the annoying Scottish vamp."

Searc ignored them both and grabbed the slacks he'd tossed to Auberi. He thrust them out. "Put them on, or we'll hogtie you and do it ourselves."

Auberi flashed a wide smile.

Malik groaned. "Stop. He looks hopeful."

"Are we doing this shit or not?" asked Blaise as he entered the hotel room, wearing black leather from head to toe. He went right to the bed and flopped onto it face first, seemingly unconcerned with Auberi being fully naked next to the very bed he was on.

"Think he realizes how close my junk is to his head?" asked Auberi.

Malik snorted. "Hell no."

"I think he's too hungover to care," said Searc.

Auberi drew upon his years of living in America and spoke in his version of an American accent. "He said *hung*."

"Dumbarse," returned Searc.

Auberi lifted his hand and flipped off the Scot. "You're the asshole, my friend. You're the one who woke me up. Not the other way around."

"You and Malik should feel honored. I only turned on the lights in yer rooms. I had to dump a bucket of ice on Blaise."

"And you're a bag of dicks for it too. All in favor of letting the bad guys go this one time?" asked Blaise, his face still planted in the bed sheets as he lifted an arm in the air.

Malik raised his hand too.

Daniel Townsend, the captain of their Crimson Op unit, entered the room next and paused, soaking in the sight of everyone gathering there. Always one to pay attention to detail, Auberi noticed Daniel's shirt straight away. It was a navy, long-sleeved shirt with pointed collars. It looked good against the medium-gray slacks he'd paired it with. "What are we voting on?"

"Nae doing our jobs," said Searc, looking somewhat unkempt in a screen-print T-shirt and a kilt. The biker boots he wore with the ensemble really drove home the fact he didn't really give a shit what anyone thought of him. He had plenty of money to buy finer things, as PSI paid extremely well, and most immortals had learned to be great with investments, but Searc didn't feel the need to be anything more than he'd been prior to being sired. Sure, his home was nice, but his wardrobe always made Auberi cringe.

Malik raised a second hand, leaving him with both arms lifted high in the air. "I'm all in on that tonight. Let someone else deal with this."

"You do nae get two votes, Tut," said Searc to Malik, calling the man the nickname they'd given him long ago because he was actually ancient Egyptian.

"I'm the only one who can walk in the sun here, so I get as many votes as I want," pressed Malik, still looking at Searc as if he wanted to murder the man for waking him. "You'd think I'd be used to how annoying you are. I work with Striker on a daily basis."

"Do nae be calling my people annoying," said Searc, defending a fellow Scotsman.

"Did we get jumped last night?" asked Blaise, his head still down flat on the bed. "Seriously, feels like my ass has been thoroughly kicked."

The last thing Auberi remembered fully was Blaise suggesting they start drinking absinthe. Clearly, that had gone better than they'd hoped. He could remember them paying extra to be permitted to simply sit at the bar drinking more and more. From there, the rest of the night was fuzzy, at best.

Auberi turned to face his friends, giving them a

full frontal, and they all glared at him. Shrugging, he took his slacks and headed for the bathroom. He was hardly bashful. "I'll remind you all that you're in my hotel room. If you don't like walking in to find me naked, do not walk in."

"Who is he kidding?" asked Malik. "He loves putting on a show."

Auberi snorted as he dressed. He brushed his teeth and then headed back out into the room and to the closet to retrieve a shirt for the night. He laid the shirt on the bed next to Blaise then went to the dresser drawer to get an undershirt and socks. He found what he was looking for, and then proceeded to finish dressing.

Daniel handed him a pair of dress shoes that went perfectly with his outfit. Had it been Blaise or Searc trying to assist him in getting ready, he'd have rejected their offer, knowing they weren't big on dressing nice. Daniel and Malik were. They, like Auberi, preferred designer clothing. Searc liked kilts. And Blaise liked looking as if he were a Goth punk and criminal.

"I hate you all," said Blaise as he lifted his head slightly, his long black hair falling into his face, covering a number of his silver piercings.

"You do nae and you know it," said Searc, clapping his hands loudly. "Let's go kill bad guys."

Malik lowered his arms. "Well, when you put it that way, I'm all in."

Auberi laughed, the idea of getting to kill things sounding good to him too. He went toward the bed and tapped Blaise's leg. "Come on, brother."

They shared a maker, making them blood brothers, even though they weren't biologically related. They'd been family to one another since the day Auberi had been sired.

Blaise had been going through something as of late, being even more reckless than normal. Pushing six hundred years old, Blaise had Auberi by more than a century, but he acted as if he was twenty at best.

Auberi, unlike most of the men they worked with, knew the truth of Blaise's past. Knew what the man had suffered through. What he'd overcome, and some of what haunted him.

Auberi had his own proverbial cross to bear with the past. His own echoes from a time long ago. A time he wished he could forget, but it didn't seem to want to leave him.

Groaning, Blaise rolled onto his back and blinked up at Auberi. "Do we gotta?"

"Yes," said Daniel sternly.

"Oh good," said Auberi snidely. "Searc's constant nitpicking and mother hen routine hasn't been enough. We really needed another parent."

Daniel lifted a brow. "You lot require multiple supervisors," he said, his British inflection coming through. "It's actually quite amazing I haven't had to hire a nanny to assist me when dealing with all of you."

"Make sure she's hot," said Blaise.

Searc sighed, his attention going to Blaise. "If you hurry, you can maybe throw beads at hot chicks who flash you their breasts."

Blaise bounced off the bed with inhuman speed. "I'm in!"

Chapter Seven

EMI CARRIED her folding table and chair as she walked into an alleyway off Jackson Square. She was used to the awkwardness the table caused when lugging it around the city, even while advertised as portable. It was still heavy when walking any type of distance, and she had walked several blocks with it, the chair, and her other supplies in tow.

She had on a backpack with her tarot cards and a tablecloth, and was ready to set up shop outside for the evening. Business had been slower than normal, but she didn't mind. It came with the territory. Her expenses were minimal on purpose. It was hard to make a living doing what she did. She lived mostly off the grid and had very little to call her own.

It was better that way.

Easier to run when the need arose.

And it had been far too long since she'd had to do so.

Her uncle would have been disappointed with her. He'd taught her to never stay in one place too long. To always stay on the move. Eight years was far too long to call one place home. Eight months would have been pushing the limits when he was still alive.

She knew that, but the idea of leaving New Orleans ripped at her gut. The city was engrained in her now, a part of her, and she a part of it. She didn't want to run anymore. She was tired. Yet, lately it felt as if the clock was ticking. That her days were numbered.

She stepped onto the stone-paved street and looked to the left to find her friend Hector. He had a canvas affixed to the iron fence there as he stood, painting for tourists to watch. Finished works of his art hung on the fence around him, on display for anyone wanting to view or purchase them. He was extremely talented and had once had a large-scale gallery showing in L.A., but had found that lifestyle wasn't for him. He'd returned to NOLA and hadn't looked back once.

She smiled as she saw him painting a mule and carriage. The mule in his painting had flowers adorning it, all done in red, and its hooves painted.

A number of mules and carriages were pulled to a stop out in front of the square, as they almost always were. Several different companies ran their carriage tours from the location, and the various drivers had to learn to coexist. Some days it was better than others.

Emi had friends who gave tours. Their love of the mules they worked with knew no bounds. They were kindhearted, loved New Orleans, and loved being able to share its rich history with people from out of town. Some even gave guided ghost tours through the Quarter. Emi had taken the tours more than once, each time seeing what others couldn't— the truth of what was in the city

While it was often filled to the brim with the living, it was always bursting at the seams with the dead. She'd know. She could see, hear, and feel them all around her. It was part of what she loved most about the area. She never felt alone. The dead were just as much her friends as the living. Often, they were even closer to her.

She couldn't recall a time in her life when she hadn't seen dead people. And she didn't remember when it was she'd developed gifts beyond those of communicating and interacting with those who had passed. It simply had always just been so. Her uncle had been able to commune with the dearly departed as well, but his gifts had been limited. No one ever came right out and said it, but it was implied that her additional gifts came from her father's side. A man who was never spoken of.

Now in her twenties, she found her gifts growing at a rate that often worried her. She'd seen far too much in her short life to believe there wasn't a price for what she'd been given, and sooner or later, her bill would come due.

She just hoped she could afford the payment.

"Hey, Emi," said Hector as he wiped his paintbrush on a tan cloth. His dark hair, which was cut close all the way around except for a portion up front, was pushed back from his face. He had on his normal jeans, white T-shirt, and a long-sleeved shirt that was cuffed to his elbows. She'd known him since her arrival in the city, and he wore a variation of the outfit daily. "You're later than usual. Everything all right?"

"I didn't get home from that house cleanse until it was nearly dawn, and then I had trouble sleeping today," she confessed, setting her table up near him. "When I finally dozed off it was midday. Slept longer than I meant to."

"Fredrick still talking your ear off?" he asked, cleaning his brush in a mason jar full of turpentine.

"He's not that bad," protested Emi. Fredrick did have a tendency to ramble when the subject was one he was passionate about, but he always had her best interests at heart. "He's my friend, and I enjoy his company."

"Taylor ever take a look at that rotting floor?" asked Hector.

She shook her head. "I never asked."

"Emi, you could get hurt. Nile and I will come over tomorrow and take a look at it."

She grinned. "I'm fine. Really."

He sighed then shook his head. "You're not fine."

She didn't really want to argue so she said nothing.

"What about Mrs. Pumpernickel?" asked Hector, changing the subject, his dark gaze knowing. He'd heard her stories enough to already know the answer to his own question.

She cringed at the mention of the ghost who tended to talk at all hours of the night when she was around. While Fredrick was a talker, he always let her get sleep. Mrs. Pumpernickel didn't really understand boundaries, or the fact Emi needed to rest. "I don't want to be rude to her, but she's having a hard time understanding that she's nearly a hundred and fifty years dead. To her, time was supposed to stop and everyone was supposed to have mourned her. I don't think they did. That hurt. I'm sure."

Hector laughed, shaking his head, having always

gotten a kick out of Emi's stories of her spirits. "She still worried her ungrateful son is going to steal all the jewels from her hidden spot?"

Nodding, Emi put her backpack on the ground and set about pulling out her dark tablecloth. "Yes. I've tried to explain that he more than likely cleaned her out long ago and that he's long dead, but she isn't having any of it. I've all but given up, and now just smile a lot when she launches into her complaints about him. Fredrick is at his wits' end with her too. And she's insistent that her jewels are still in the home."

"I always feel bad for the ones that don't understand how long they've been gone," Hector said.

"It's worse when they don't even know they're dead," she confessed, having run into more than her fair share of spirits who had no idea they were even dead. Telling them was always a touchy matter and could end in disaster. Some took it well, but others threw the mother of all tantrums.

"I bet," said Hector. He never judged her and her abilities. He'd accepted what she could do on faith when they'd first met, and always expressed a genuine concern for her well-being. It was just part of what she liked about him. In a way, he and the others she'd met while reading cards in NOLA had become her family of sorts. "I wish I had a way to shut that off for you for a while. You deserve a break too."

"Thank you." She wasn't sure what life would be like if she had a day without a spirit appearing in it. Part of her thought it would probably feel like she was walking naked through life. Another part of her longed for the experience, even if just once.

She set her cards on the table and was about to open her chair when two women approached. They were dressed in shorts, T-shirts, and tennis shoes. They had saddlebags that were slung over their shoulders and looked to be stuffed to the gills with items that would appeal to tourists. The woman on the left was incredibly fair-skinned and had evidently spent far too long in the NOLA heat and sun. Her face was beet red, as was her upper chest, her arms, and the front of her legs. She'd be miserable once she realized how badly she was sunburned.

The other wasn't burnt, but she did look as if the heat and humidity were getting to her. Her forehead was coated in a sheen of sweat, and her hair looked as though she'd been pushing said sweat into it for some time. It was evident that neither woman was local.

"Can you read our cards?" asked the sunburned one, a British accent evident.

Emi offered a warm smile. "I can."

Hector brought over an extra chair for her, and she nodded her thanks to him. He and his husband, Nile—a stock trader who did very well for himself—were always looking out for her. Whenever a group of men got too rowdy near Emi's table, or if one tried to put the moves on her, Hector always made his presence known, as if he was her protector.

In truth, Emi could more than handle herself. It made Hector happy to watch over her so she permitted it, never once letting on that she could take matters into her own hands and deal with them accordingly.

Chapter Eight

THOR WALKED DOWN BOURBON STREET, doing his best to ignore the nauseating smells surrounding him. His senses were far superior to those of the humans around him, meaning he could smell and hear everything happening not only in the immediate area but farther out. He could smell everything from truck exhaust to horse shit. The area had it all.

His senses had been on overdrive since his arrival in the city. Normally, he was good at zeroing in and blocking out the unwanted. The bombardment of information coming at him from all angles was nearly too much. He had to close his eyes a moment to gather his thoughts and concentrate on blocking everything that was coming at him at once.

The area was body to body with people, and it

wasn't even the busy season in the French Quarter. That didn't seem to matter to everyone who had jammed into the area that only extended something like thirteen blocks in one direction and nine blocks in the other direction.

It was hot and the extra bodies only made the area hotter. The summer heat left sweat trickling down his back. The weather only added to the stench of the French Quarter, baking the trash that sat out in plastic bins. Sadly, the trash smelled better than the vomit and piss that filled the area, and it wasn't for lack of the city trying to clean the streets.

If the humans visiting there treated the place better, it wouldn't smell as bad as it did.

His lip curled.

Humans thought they could come to the city and behave any way they wanted. They drank to the point they could barely stand and then relieved themselves against the buildings like animals.

No. Animals are better.

He'd know. After all, he had the ability to shift into a panther.

A group of drunk men came rushing out of a bar, yelling and throwing their hands in the air in celebration. From what little Thor could make out from their drunken ramblings, it was one of the men's bachelor parties. From the looks of it, they were doing their best to make it a night no one would remember come morning. Not one of them appeared to be even semi-sober.

Morons.

It was no wonder crime was on the rise in the area. Tourists were too shit-faced to realize they were being marked for theft. He would never fully understand how anyone thought getting so drunk they vomited was an enjoyable night out. What kind of crap life did they have that they looked forward to doing that to themselves?

At least they have a life.

He stiffened. It was true. His life was spent in the service of Pierre. And it was no picnic. Maybe the men who could barely hold their liquor, and would no doubt contribute to the urine smell soon enough, had the right idea.

Thor had his blond hair pulled back into a tie at the nape of his neck. The black short-sleeve shirt he wore began to cling to his back. As he continued down the street, he realized his choice of clothing looked a great deal like that of a number of the bouncers he passed. Black shirt, black pants, black boots.

Though none of the bouncers looked lethal. He was.

He'd waited until the sun had started to set before he'd ventured out from the high-end apartment Pierre had secured for his stay, in search of his mark. Unlike most of the master's creations, Thor could tolerate sunlight to some degree. Though he found it bothered his eyes and drained him the longer he was in full sun. He didn't burst into flames like the pure vampires did, nor did his skin begin to bubble and burn like that of some of the hybrid creations.

He was different from them in other ways too. And he'd thought he was sane in comparison, but his nightly dreams and constant urge to want to kill his maker said otherwise. Perhaps he, like the others, was shattering mentally. It seemed to happen to them all.

He faltered in his step, coming to a stop and doing his best to remain calm. Panicking over the state of his mental health wouldn't help in the least. He'd seen the spiral other hybrids had taken. Some had seen the end coming and lived in paranoid fear of it, only serving to drive themselves mad sooner. Others never knew what was happening to them. They didn't understand how broken they were.

Which was he?

And who would hunt him when he finally snapped fully?

Would Pierre delight in getting to take down his prized pet?

The fact he was now tasked with a mission Pierre felt was of the utmost importance said the man still held trust for Thor, but it was impossible to tell how much. Pierre had never used him for sex and blood, as he did a number of his pets. Though Thor was confident that was the end goal of the master. The hungry look Pierre held whenever Thor was in his presence worried him. It was only a matter of time before Pierre demanded more than Thor was willing to give.

Already Thor refused to follow the man's orders blindly. He should want to do whatever the man commanded, but that wasn't the case. It had never been the case.

I am broken.

His mind was slipping, as was clear by his obsession with the name Lance, and his fear of sleeping. Soon he would be the prey, instead of the hunter. Pierre had dispatched him on numerous occasions over the last year to track down a creation that had snapped. And now he was tasked with hunting the enforcer that Pierre's direct competition used.

Gérard Voclain had a large foothold in the southern part of Louisiana. When Thor had first awoken as one of Pierre's children, he'd thought Gérard and Pierre were friends. Within a few short weeks, Thor came to understand that Pierre had no friends. He had people whom he used and kept close to suit his needs. Nothing more.

And now Gérard had served his need. Pierre

wanted his territory. To achieve that, Gérard's henchmen needed to be removed from the equation. That was where Thor came in. He was to track Gérard's right-hand man, Chilton, and kill him, but not before he found out what had drawn the man to the city to begin with. There was something of interest to him here, and Pierre wanted to know what that was. If it could be used to gain the upper hand in the war that was waging with the operatives, so be it.

Thor understood the mission.

Chilton and Thor had had run-ins more than once in the past. There was always much in the way of posturing whenever the two alpha-male enforcers were in the same room. To date, they'd not gone to blows, but that was coming soon enough.

Chilton was said to be living in New Orleans, hiding among the eccentrics in the Crescent City. It wouldn't be hard for a creature of the night to thrive in the area. Dating back to its inception, the city was rich with lore of vampires, shifters, witches and more inhabiting the region, calling NOLA home.

Thor knew the stories of New Orleans, or *La Nouvelle-Orléans*, as it had originally been known, and had a deep understanding that he'd been in the area many times before, yet his ability to recall details was gone. When he'd woke, reborn as one of the master's pets, his past was blank. All he'd known was Pierre's face, his commanding tone, and the desire to obey. Yet that desire had waned quickly, and Thor had been wise enough to know that letting on to as much would prove to be deadly.

He stepped out into the street, walking around a group of tourists who were swept up in the happenings on Bourbon Street. He watched a man do a shot from a woman's breasts at the entrance to a bar, all the while the other woman with the man clapped and laughed. The man appeared incredibly uncomfortable with the act but continued all the same. The woman handing out the shot looked happy enough to have ten dollars in hand for the shot. She moved on to the next tourist, coaxing him to do a shot from her breasts as well. That man didn't agree to drink from her breasts but he did let her hold the shot in her mouth, choosing instead to take it from her that way.

Whatever works for the guy.

Continuing onward, Thor stepped around a street performer dressed to look like he was a vampire, cape and all. A set of fake fangs was in the man's mouth, making it hard to understand him when he spoke. It was nearly laughable, but the tourists seemed to enjoy it. Many were gathered around the man, getting photos with him as he spoke with a campy B-movie actor voice.

"Come, my children," he said, really hamming it up for the tourist. "And I will show you my lair. Fear not, humans, I only bite…a little."

The people around him laughed as if the joke was really funny.

Thor entertained showing them all real fangs but held back. They'd probably wet themselves and he'd be left having to smell even more urine on the street. He avoided doing what he wanted, despite wanting to scare them more than he should. A darkness in him, no doubt driven by his vampire side, wanted to cause chaos. Wanted screaming and running in fear.

The man—though he wasn't sure he had much left inside him—fought against it. He felt the human portion of him deep down, struggling to suppress the blood hunger, the need for destruction.

He trembled, the fear of becoming the same monster Pierre was hitting him hard. Would he find joy in others' agony, as Pierre did? Or would he far surpass Pierre's coldness?

Sweat dripped down his forehead and into his eye, burning it enough to help him gather control of himself once more—something he found himself doing often. He was thankful for the heat then. It had saved him from falling victim to his own demon.

He would have continued onward on his mission

to locate Chilton, but a strange feeling came over him.

Thor paused, glancing around, unsure if there was a threat nearby or not. It was as if his body was torn between being ready for an attack and prepared for bliss. What an odd pairing. He knew it couldn't be coming from Chilton, as Thor's only response to the man had been repulsion and the urge to rip the asshole's head off. And since Thor didn't feel any of those things, he felt fairly certain it wasn't Chilton, or any of Gérard's men, for that matter. But it was something more than merely human.

Humans didn't ever trip his inner alarms or sensors. They weren't something he felt the need to be on high alert for. There was no denying the power wafting through the air around him. It ran over his body, wrapping around it, arousing him.

Yeah, that sure the fuck isn't Chilton.

His gaze darted up to the balconies and galleries, perched above the street, all nods to the French and Spanish architecture of the area. They were filled with people. Some were sitting and enjoying libations, others were standing and shouting down at those on the street below. None were the source of the power though. He'd have sensed it if they were.

The power drifted away as quickly as it had come.

What the hell am I doing on this wild-goose chase?

He was walking aimlessly around a huge city, hoping to what, bump into the damn enemy? He'd had better ideas. Much better. But he'd been desperate to put distance between himself and his master. He'd latched on to the assignment, jumping at the chance to hunt and kill Chilton, but he didn't know where the vampire was in the city, or what he was up to. Pierre had had little information to go off of regarding finding Chilton or the secret weapon Gérard was rumored to possess. Pierre didn't even know why they were in the city. Yet, he expected Thor to be able to hunt down and eliminate the threat.

"Easy as fucking pie," said Thor, partially under his breath.

He came to another stop and tapped into his sensitive hearing, doing his best to focus his attention and filter out the overwhelming amount of information coming at him. The Quarter was the hub of the city. If Chilton was in town and up to no good, chances were, someone here would know about it. Thor just had to figure out who that someone might be.

Thor filtered out everything around him that

wasn't relevant to his mission. It took a few seconds, but it worked.

"Did you hear they found a body last night, just outside of the Quarter?" asked a woman, her voice thick with a Louisiana drawl.

"That is the fourth one in a week," said another woman, sounding like she was from the north.

Thor visually scanned the direction from which he'd zeroed in on the voices. He spotted two women standing just outside of a bar. Each was smoking cigarettes and had on matching T-shirts with the bar's name on them. Both were fake blondes and had equally fake breasts. They weren't bad-looking, yet he found they didn't appeal to him sexually. He wasn't sure what his type was, but they weren't it.

The taller of the two leaned in close, keeping her voice low. "Something is hunting around here at night."

"Non-human?" asked the other, surprising Thor. They knew of supernaturals? He could smell the humanity rolling off them.

"My friend, the cop, said it looked like the body was eaten by a pack of wolves or something." The woman flicked her cigarette onto the ground and then stepped on it, her heeled foot snuffing it out. "Don't walk home or anything. Get a ride from one of the bouncers or the bartenders, okay?"

"Yeah," said the other woman. "Should we spread the word?"

"Yes, but keep it to those we trust. We don't want the tourists running off," said the taller one. "As of right now, it's not hunting any of them."

The shorter of the two nodded and then walked into the crowd on the street. Thor followed, shadowing her from a distance as she entered another bar and then came out, heading to a restaurant. She exited there and soon found a group of men standing together.

"Guys, there was another attack last night," she said.

The oldest of the men sighed. "Anyone we know?"

"I don't know who it was yet. But it was bad. I'm gonna go tell the others. Can you spread the word about it on the down low?" she asked.

"Of course, Cherry," he said. "Do you want one of us to walk you home tonight?"

She smiled and then hugged him. "Thank you. But I'll be fine."

The men didn't look as if they agreed with her statement, but she continued onward.

Thor soaked in what he'd learned. Something was hunting locals and odds were, it was tied to why he was in the city. It was no secret that Gérard had been in talks with Krauss and The Corporation.

Both had hard-ons for genetic engineering and messing with DNA. Thor should have held Krauss in higher regard than he did, as the man had given him to Pierre and saved his life, but he'd never been able to shake the feeling that Krauss wasn't trustworthy and should be destroyed.

He's a pimple on a dog's ass.

While in Seattle, Thor had seen firsthand the results of the genetic testing going sideways. He'd stood face to face with true monsters in every sense of the word. They weren't to be toyed with. They were feral.

Much like most of Pierre's attempts at creating the perfect pets—the perfect hybrids. Even Thor's mind was beginning to slip. Soon, another would have to come along and hunt him, putting him out of his misery.

Chapter Nine

EMI STOOD from her table and walked over to Hector, who was lost in his art, as was often the case. She envied the way he could shut off everything around him and simply paint. That wasn't a skill set she had, though it was one she'd always longed for. The idea of having a hobby—something other than reading fortunes, cleansing houses, and sitting and chatting it up with dead people—was a foreign concept to her. Those things had been her life. All she'd ever known. And her life didn't exactly leave a lot of wiggle room or spare time. If it did, she wasn't even sure what she'd do with it. Cook, maybe. She'd always loved the few times she and her uncle had lived in places with a kitchen.

Missing her uncle, she touched her chest lightly while she got lost in watching Hector paint. It was somewhat therapeutic the way his hand moved with each brush stroke.

As night wore on, the crowds around them began to change as well. They became rowdier. Such was always the case on the Quarter. She didn't mind it. In fact, it often amused her the way some people carried on.

She'd done several readings, making a nice chunk of money that she'd store away in her safe spot. Hoarding cash was engrained in her. If she had to run, it would get her somewhere safe and afford her the opportunity to start anew. The very idea of leaving those who had become family to her in New Orleans caused her breath to hitch.

Hector glanced at her and then motioned to his artwork. "What do you think?"

"I love it! It won't last long before someone buys it." It was true. Hector was a tourist favorite. He'd start the process of packing up soon enough because of how dark it was. "What would you like to eat tonight?"

"Hot dogs?" he asked, looking hopeful. He had a thing for the specialty hot dogs that were sold just across the Quarter at a small restaurant. She didn't mind them either. They were some of her favorite foods.

"Sounds good."

He began to clean his brush. "I'll go get them."

"No. Your muse is on fire tonight. That is some of your best work yet. I'll go," she offered. "You finish up. Besides, you worked longer than normal tonight and your takedown process will keep you busy until I get back."

He gave her a hard look. "Fine, but I'm buying."

She went to him and kissed his cheek. "Thank you."

"Where's Taylor? He typically comes by wanting our food order by now," Hector said. "And are we checking in on Cherry to see if she wants something to eat too?"

Putting her tarot cards in her bag, Emi glanced around, wanting to be sure no one overheard before she told Hector where Taylor was. Austin had a number of people in the Quarter who were loyal to him. Eyes and ears all over the place. It was sad what some people would do for the promise of drugs. And Austin was never in short supply of them. He made a good amount of money running scams on tourists and selling drugs. He wasn't the type of guy people tangled with on purpose. She didn't need or want issues with Austin's crew tonight. "Taylor left for Colorado today. He wants to be close to his sister when she has her baby, and I'm pretty sure he wants to mend fences with his past."

Hector looked impressed. "You finally managed to talk him away from that group of miscreants. Good."

She laughed, already knowing Hector's low opinion of the friends Taylor had associated with before coming to live with her. Hector was part of a group of small-business owners who were trying to get Austin and his crew off the streets and out of the city. For a while, others like Austin had been driven out, but new ones had cropped up, and they were far worse than the ones before. "I'm dreading them realizing he's left the city."

Hector's gaze hardened. "If those punks come near you, I'll…"

She snickered. "You'll what? Throw paint thinner at them?"

Hector grinned from ear to ear. "Hey, paint-brushes could be used as a weapon. You'd be shocked at how kick-ass I can be when called for."

"My hero," she said, touching her chest in an old-movie, Southern-belle kind of way and then making a move to leave to get their food. "I'll stop by and see if Cherry wants some too."

"Emi," he said sternly.

She faced him, and he held out money, waving it around. "I told you I was buying. Put Cherry's on there too."

She took the cash from him. "Fine. You want your usual?"

"Yes, darling, and thank you," he said, kissing her forehead gently. "Hurry back, or I'll think Austin and his crew found you. You do not want to know the hell I'd unleash on him if he hurts you."

She snorted. "I'm sure he's terrified."

Hector winked.

She smiled and headed in the direction of the hot dog place. It was a bit of a walk because it was on the opposite side of the Quarter, but she didn't mind. She walked nearly everywhere she went, and used street-cars or RTA buses when the distance was too far to walk. New Orleans provided everything she needed to live a simple life and she'd had a great love for the city since her arrival. It was filled to the brim with spirits, most of whom were good and loved the city as much as her. Some were not so nice. She ignored them. No matter what, it had become her home. A part of her.

It was the longest she'd ever spent in one area, and she hoped to be able to remain for at least a while longer. She couldn't imagine living anywhere else and leaving the tribe of friends she'd created in the area. They were the closest thing to a family she had.

She strolled in the direction of Bourbon Street to seek out her friend Cherry and get her food order. Cherry had a soft spot for hot dogs as well. Emi didn't mind the extra walk.

As she stepped out onto Bourbon Street to head down to the bar Cherry worked at, the urge to look to her right came over her. She did—and froze.

There was a man standing there, his gaze upward as if he was scanning the rooftops. His long blond hair was pulled back from his face, and he wore black from head to toe, from his form-fitting T-shirt, to his painted-on jeans, to the boots that screamed badass. His outfit showed off every ripple of his chiseled body.

Her mouth went dry as she found herself standing in the street, soaking in the sight of the man. He wasn't even facing her and she knew he was sheer perfection.

Men simply didn't come built that way in real life, did they? She had to be imagining him.

An even more sobering thought occurred to her —was he dead?

A few times in her life, she'd been unable to easily discern the difference between the living and the dead. Some dead were simply so unique that they came across to her as living, yet something always felt slightly off with them.

As was the case with the man.

He felt alive, yet not.

It was an odd pairing, and it intrigued her. Not

to mention he was the hottest guy she'd ever seen, and it wasn't as if she'd spent her life running into slackers. But none of the men before could hold a candle to the sexy hunk of man meat that was still watching the skies like he expected them to open at any moment.

As she watched him, she noticed spirits on the street being drawn to him as well. Often it was her they sought, but not now. They were drawn to the man, just as she was.

Strange.

She couldn't tear her gaze from him. For a split second, she realized she was watching him as if he were soft-core porn. As guilty as she should have felt over objectifying the man, she found she didn't want to stop. Truth be told, she wanted to get him naked and objectify him some more.

Right and wrong didn't even come into play.

Emi wanted to be closer to him. Wanted to see if he smelled as yummy as he looked. That was so out of character for her that it should have jarred her back to her senses. It didn't.

He moved a few paces, and she remained there, watching him, mesmerized by his sheer presence. The man's movements reminded her of a cat—smooth and fluid. He held himself in a way that said he wasn't to be messed with. That he could hold his own should the need call for it. And she still wasn't able to figure out why it was she sensed both life and death on him. It was far more than the feeling she got around someone who'd had a life-and-death experience. More than the vibe she pulled from someone who had crossed over temporarily into death, only to live another day. This was more. Darker, yet scarily so.

He turned slightly. She'd been right. Sheer perfection. He was quite possibly the sexiest man she'd ever laid eyes on. His features looked to be carved from stone, the angles of his face the perfect ratio. His blue gaze was crisp and captivating. There was something about the man that screamed Nordic god.

Her hormones did a happy dance, rejoicing in simply being on the same street as the hunk. She wasn't sure they could handle anything more. While she'd never before considered herself the type of woman who caved and gave in to carnal urges, she was fast beginning to see why so many women did. With a guy as sexy as the blond, she wasn't sure how much longer she could hold out.

He stopped looking upward and began to scan the area surrounding him as if he sensed a threat. Whatever was stupid enough to try to harm him wouldn't last long. Emi could almost feel the alpha in the man as it pulsed from him. While Hector was all talk, this man would be all show. She was sure of it.

His gaze narrowed partially on a group of men who were walking in his direction. The men took one look at the blond, and they all walked wide around him, giving him plenty of space.

They felt it too.

The danger that rolled off the man.

That being said, she wasn't afraid of him. If anything, she felt drawn to him. Like she needed to walk in his direction, to be closer to him. To simply be in his radius even. As if he were the sun and she a planet needing to orbit it. Never before had she had a compulsion such as this. She wasn't sure how she felt about it. Curious for one, but for another, slightly scared of the intense physical reaction she had to the man. What did it mean?

She made a point to avoid relationships, or even casual sex. The very few times in her past that she'd tried to be sexually intimate with someone had ended poorly. Her ability to read their pasts, presents, and futures always got in the way. What was worse was when they had dead people attached to them. Having a private moment to get it on with a spirit watching her wasn't something she found alluring.

The more she stared at the blond guy, the more she realized she didn't care if a stadium full of the departed wanted to watch. Emi wanted him. Period. Never before had she felt anything close to what she was feeling now. She wanted to run her fingers over the hard planes of his body to see if he was as hard as he looked.

I bet he feels better, she thought, absently running her tongue out and over her lower lip. *And I bet he's really friggin' hard.*

Melting into a puddle of hormones felt as if it were a real possibility. One she'd never considered a threat before, but as the temperature around her seemed to rise and her lady parts rejoiced at the sight of the hunk, she wasn't so sure anymore.

The urge to seek out Cherry hit her. Cherry was something of an expert when it came to men. Emi was anything but, and the hunk before her looked like he'd more than know what he was doing in the bedroom. Emi felt like she needed a crash course in how to please and handle a sex god.

She gulped at the idea of sleeping with the man. If the very idea of it was causing her body to react in such a way, would she survive the real thing?

Nope.

Someone bumped into her, ripping her from thoughts of throwing herself at the blond guy and begging him to do her hard. Instead, the urge was replaced with an onslaught of images and feelings. She'd worked hard to learn to control her gifts and avoid information overload from touching another. Her focus had been so swept up with the man that she'd let her mystical defenses down, opening herself to a barrage of emotions and visions.

She swayed, feeling instantly sick to her stomach. The woman who had run into her reached out and touched Emi's arm, using Emi to partially steady herself. The act made more information collide with Emi, slamming into and through her to the point it was painful.

Her uncle's teachings came back to her quickly and she did as she'd been taught when she was little and it was all new. She began to hum slightly, focusing on the song in her head, not the images and feelings of another. It helped, just as it had long ago.

"S-s-orry," the woman slurred, smelling heavily of booze.

Emi blinked several times and drew upon her hard-earned skills to block impressions from others. Once the images in her head subsided, she pressed an artificial smile to her face. "It's okay."

The woman continued onward. The man she was with looped his arm through hers, keeping her close and upright. Something many seemed to struggle with in the Quarter after hours.

Emi moved to the sidewalk and stood under a balcony, continuing to watch the man who had caught her attention. His gaze was still skimming the crowded street. Whatever he was looking for, he hadn't found it yet, but he'd certainly drawn an audience of the dearly departed. He seemed totally unaware of their presence.

Chapter Ten

THOR CONTINUED to look around Bourbon Street, sensing the alluring power nearby. It was far more intense than it had been, as if it was much closer. All he knew for sure was, it tugged at his gut, demanding his full attention. He needed to locate the source, which he was fast beginning to suspect was female, yet he couldn't shake the feeling the energy had similar undertones to the power he'd felt coming from Gérard and Chilton in the past. Whatever was near was powerful, yet it wasn't a threat to him.

He stared up at the rooftops, knowing a large number of supernaturals could make easy work of traveling through the Quarter by way of them. There was nothing out of the ordinary there. Yet he still felt the presence of something supernatural close to him. It was close enough to have eyes on him, he was sure of that.

He turned in a slow circle, his gaze narrowing on a group of men walking in his direction. His alpha side flared to the surface, daring them to come closer. Wisely, they veered off, heading wide and into the street more to avoid walking too close.

Smart boys.

And they were boys compared to him. While he didn't look much older than his mid-twenties, he knew deep down that he was far older than that. He just didn't know how much. For all he knew, he could be a thousand. He knew Pierre was several hundred years old, but didn't look any older than thirty. It was possible that Thor was as old or older than that even.

Though he highly doubted Pierre would have sired him, had that been the case. The older a supernatural was, the stronger they tended to be. There were always exceptions to the rule, but that was generally the case. And Pierre wasn't a fan of being the lesser of the species.

You could take him, he thought, wondering if he really could. Thor was something Pierre wasn't—a hybrid. And that meant he was strong.

Very fucking strong.

There was also the fact that he wasn't limited to moving around only at night, like Pierre. He knew where Pierre slept during the daylight hours, and how to get around the security in place around the man—security Thor helped to implement.

Yes, you could take him.

He stopped daydreaming about ending his maker's existence and started looking around again for the source of the disturbance that he'd felt. He needed to know who the source of the power was. He couldn't explain why. The longer he stood there, trying to zero in on the source, the more he realized that he wasn't just aroused by the power, it was now carrying its own telltale signs of desire as well. And it most certainly was female.

His entire body lit with need.

He focused in on the women near him, trying to figure out which, if any, of them, were the source of the power. A group of young women stood in the center of the street and flashed their breasts at men above. The men all yelled in appreciation and began throwing plastic beaded necklaces down to the women, who already had quite a collection. Each woman looked more intoxicated than the next, and all seemed to take great joy in their antics as they encouraged one another to flash the men again.

A buxom brunette held her shirt up and shook her upper body, making her breasts bounce wildly.

The sight did nothing for him. The women in the group weren't tied to the alluring power.

He certainly wouldn't be thinking of them when he jerked off next. He knew he could bed any or all of the women in the group if he wanted to. They'd come with him willingly and enjoy every second of pleasure he provided. He didn't need his memories to be sure of that much. It was simply ingrained in him.

And while they were all more than passable by any man's standards, they didn't make his cock stir. They didn't make his body burn with desire. Not like the woman he'd imagined when he'd been in the shower, stroking himself.

Stop waiting for a fantasy. Find a hot chick and bang her. It could help jog your memory.

His nostrils flared at the idea of taking any of the loose-moraled women to bed. He'd seek out another female and use her to sate his manly needs. But first, he'd track the source of the pull he felt. The keeper of the power that danced over the night air like a light-footed nymph sent forth to tempt the untemptable.

Thor was about to move on down the street more, hoping to catch a scent or feeling that would help him track what he'd felt, when the smell of lavender and sage wafted over him, riding the power. Instantly, his mind went back to the fantasy woman he'd thought of while pleasuring himself. For a moment, images of her flashed through his mind so rapidly that he could focus on little else.

Oh God, he thought, panic rising. *I'm finally snapping. This is it. This is my breaking point.*

He lifted his hands and touched his temples in a pathetic attempt to stave off the snapping of his mind. He'd hunted far too many broken hybrids to think for a moment he had a snowball's chance in hell of holding back the tides of insanity. Yet still, he tried. Desperate times called for desperate measures.

He looked past the group of women who were still showing their chests for beads—and froze, his hands still up, his fingers still pressed to his temples.

There, through the throngs of bodies, was the very woman who had flashed through his mind when he was jerking off. The fantasy woman. The woman he'd envisioned while in the shower.

Was she really there or merely a figment of his imagination? A final glimpse of something beautiful before his mind broke completely, leaving him a raving madman who hunted and killed everything around him for the sheer pleasure of the sport?

No!

Again, the scent of lavender mixed with sage came to him, surfing the wave of power he'd been tracking, calming him to a degree. Was this his body's way of accepting the inevitable?

He exhaled and lowered his hands from his head, his gaze still locked on the woman that he wasn't even sure was truly there.

It wasn't until he saw a man step around the dark-haired beauty that he realized she might not be a symptom of a psychotic break. She just might be real. People didn't step around things that weren't there.

Did they?

For a split second, Thor's vision tunneled in on her, as if she were the only other person on Bourbon Street with him. The vampire side of him took instant note of the sound of her blood beating through her veins, another sign she was real. His fangs nearly broke free from his gums as if they could already taste her. And the shifter side of him fought to push forward from within, wanting free to explore her, bury its head in her sex and memorize her scent before licking every fucking inch of her. The very thought of it all nearly had him losing his shit and coming in his jeans in the middle of the street.

Mine, he nearly snarled out loud.

Gone was the stench of the city, replaced only by the woman's scent—sage and lavender. The same scent he'd smelled when thinking of her as he'd stroked himself in the shower. As he drew in a deeper breath, his cock responded, hardening at once, making his jeans uncomfortable. The urge to adjust himself was great, but he resisted, too frozen in rapture with the woman to do anything but stare in her direction. It *was* her. The very woman he'd envisioned while pleasuring himself in the shower. The same women he'd pictured each time he'd touched himself for the last several months.

She was real.

How could that be? And what were the odds that he'd not only discover the woman he fantasized about was real, but in New Orleans the same time he was?

He tensed, remembering Belial, and how Pierre had sent the broken shell of a man after who later turned out to be his own sister. The goal all along had been to have Belial try to kill his sister. It was a game to Pierre. He'd been more than willing to sacrifice one of his pets as a pawn, all to get the girl. And if the girl couldn't be captured and couldn't best Belial, Pierre had wanted her killed.

This had shades of the master's past trickery. It would explain why Pierre had been sketchy on the details surrounding the mission in NOLA, and why he'd sent Thor on what seemed like a wild-goose chase.

Was he playing with Thor? Was this a twisted form of torture to punish him for refusing to conform fully to the dark gift given to him and for helping the Ops so much recently?

Did Pierre know something from Thor's past that he was using against him now? Did Pierre want to toy with him by putting a woman Thor knew from his past life—before being sired—within reach, only to have her killed?

No! his demon and his shifter sides roared in unison.

She would not be harmed. He would unleash a hell the likes of which the world had never seen if she was hurt in any way.

A sickening thought hit him hard, making him step back, his gaze still on the woman. What if the master had orchestrated events in such a way that Thor, himself, would be the woman's end? What if he was the ultimate threat to the female before him?

No!

The vampire and the panther in him came to an understanding. He would not hurt her. No one would harm her. She was to be protected at all costs. If Pierre was scheming with the hopes of something happening to the woman, Thor would tear the fucker's head off himself. The master wouldn't have to wait for an enemy to strike. Thor would be his end, because deep down Thor knew without a shadow of a doubt, that this woman would be his salvation.

The beautiful woman at the center of his fixation stood there, her arms folded under her chest, her long dark brown hair pulled back from her face with a red scarf that wrapped around her head. She wore a flowing yellow and red peasant skirt that stopped at mid-calf, and wooden beaded necklaces and bracelets. Her tank top was a pale yellow, drawing attention to her covered chest and offsetting her tanned skin.

She was even more breathtaking in person. He wasn't sure how that was possible. Yet there she was, in the flesh, making his body burn with need. She was stunning, her brown gaze soaking in the sights before her while she remained removed from it all— untouched by the raunchiness and rowdiness surrounding her. She was like an angel in brightly colored clothing.

Two men, each in a competition to look more unkempt than the next, approached the beauty at a rapid speed. From the looks on their faces, they not only knew her, they were none too pleased with her.

They intend her harm.

The panther and the vampire sides of Thor rose from within, wanting him to shift into a hybrid form that was neither fully beast, nor fully vampire. It was lethal and without mercy. Neither side gave a rat's ass that he was in the center of a crowded street, with tourists and cell phones that recorded video everywhere.

The darkness in him wanted to rip the men's heads from their shoulders and then celebrate over their rotting corpses. The closer the vagabonds got to the woman, the harder Thor found it was to control his darkness. It beat at him from within like a drum from hell, wanting to be heard no matter the cost.

Red haze began to filter into the edges of his vision. He zeroed in on the males, hyper-focusing on them. Their scent was rank, and it smelled as if neither had bathed in weeks. The heavy smell of drugs came from them, in addition to alcohol and simple body odor. The male in the front, with matted medium-brown hair, narrowed his gaze more on the woman, the muscles in his jaw tightening, a sign he was going to attack.

As he whispered "bitch," Thor shut off.

Thor broke through the bodies on the street before him and was nearly to the men, when suddenly they came to a grinding halt. The man in the lead looked as if he'd slammed into something that wasn't there—an invisible force. Jerking, the man righted himself and attempted to go for the woman again.

Thor gave in to his rage, unable to deny his darkness what it wanted. He charged the men and passed through something that could only be described as a wall of power. It had the slightest of burns to it that faded quickly, allowing him to pass without further incident. In an instant, he was face to face with the disgusting-smelling men. He glared down at the one who had intended to harm the female.

The man actually looked as if he wanted to try to take on Thor. Suddenly, Thor wasn't sure who was the crazy one—him, or the guy who thought he might stand a chance against him. The idea of the man-child being able to hold a candle to him nearly made Thor laugh. He would have found amusement in it if the man hadn't been threatening his woman.

My woman?

"Austin?" asked the other guy. Fear was evident in the man's voice.

Austin narrowed his gaze on Thor. "We've got no beef with you, man. Step aside. The bitch has got some shit to answer for."

The bitch?

Oh, it was clear the man wanted his tongue ripped from his head. Thor was just the guy to do it. Unable to form words, Thor bared his teeth, knowing they were partially shifted, leaving him with dangerous-looking fangs.

Austin's face paled, and he backed up, nearly falling. The man behind him caught him, keeping him upright.

Thor wanted to shed their blood. To bathe in it as a warning to anyone thinking of harming the woman. Come near her and perish. The concept was simple. She was not to be harmed.

Period.

Death awaited any who tried.

Chapter Eleven

A SMALL HAND touched Thor's upper back lightly, drawing him slightly from the fierce need to kill. Heat flared through him. It caught him so off guard that he nearly did a full shift then and there in the middle of Bourbon Street. It didn't matter that people were all around him. All that mattered was the tender touch, the heat, the desire.

The woman he'd been captivated by eased around him, her hand skimming his back and then his upper arm. She came to a stop next to him, coming to his chin. He realized in that moment how perfectly their bodies would fit together, and he wanted to be locked together with her, sinking into her silken depths, finding release.

Her scent washed over him, taking more of his rage and dousing it marginally. Finally able to cage his beast, Thor went perfectly still, afraid she'd stop touching him. Making contact with her made him feel alive. More alive than he'd felt in all the time that he could recall. He didn't want it to end.

Ever.

She kept her hand on his arm and tugged slightly, going to her tiptoes in the process. She radiated peace and calming energy, something he sorely lacked at the moment.

Thor retracted his fangs and relaxed, craving her touch. He kept his gaze locked on the men, daring them to try to harm the woman again. He didn't care who was watching. He'd kill them then and there.

Fuck the consequences.

The men righted themselves but kept a close eye on Thor. Austin pushed on his friend's chest. "Did you see his teeth?"

"Dude, what is your damage?" asked the other man. "We came here to teach Emi a lesson about interfering where she doesn't belong."

Emi.

The beauty's name fit her well.

Thor growled, the sound low and deep. "No one touches her."

The men shared a look then backed up more.

The braver of the two looked to the woman. "Emi, we know you're the one who talked Taylor into leaving. He owes us money and he took what was ours. This isn't over."

Thor made a move to go at the man but Emi tugged harder. Thor glanced at her. "He threatened you."

"He doesn't scare me," she said, remaining perfectly calm, though he noticed something else beginning to come from her as well… Was it desire?

Thor couldn't look away from her. She was simply that breathtaking. "I could make their deaths quick."

Her lips twitched. "Uh, thanks, but let's not kill anyone, okay?"

He merely watched her. "If that's what you want, but the offer stands."

"Fuck you, asshole," said the man with Austin.

Thor focused on him, letting his beast up slightly.

Austin pulled on the man and continued to back up. He ran into a blockage, cutting off a portion of both the sidewalk and the street for construction. Out of places to retreat, he jerked on his friend and pulled him into the street. "Let's go."

"But we said we were gonna…" The man's words died off as Austin practically dragged him in the opposite direction.

Thor remained in place, paralyzed by the

woman's touch. He wanted her hands to skim lower —over his groin, to be exact.

She eased around him more, standing in front of him fully. Her large brown eyes seemed to look right through him, and he found himself getting lost in them.

She's not the mission.

Still, he couldn't tear his gaze from hers. He knew her. Knew those eyes, those lips, that body. He could almost taste how sweet her cream would be. Like he already knew.

She reached up with her other hand to touch his face, and he stiffened. Her fingers moved over his cheek tenderly. She closed her eyes and rocked in place, leaning into him slightly. His hands found her hips as if they had minds of their own. He drew her closer as she continued to touch his face, her eyes remaining closed.

Thor's hands could have met around her tiny waist if he tried. He didn't like how thin she was. The need to sweep her up, take her away and feed her was great. But he didn't want to move too much, fearing he'd chase her away. The moment was one he didn't want to end. He could stand there forever, touching her and her touching him, the moment was that perfect.

He closed his eyes and lowered his head, inhaling her scent. His body responded once again, leaving no room for doubt that he was attracted to her. He wanted her in a way he'd wanted nothing else. Just having her close nearly made him come. It was as if his body was trained to respond to hers.

Was it?

When he opened his eyes, he found her staring up at him, a look of wonder on her face. Thor could do nothing more than look at her, noticing the tiny flecks of green sprinkled through her brown eyes. The more he looked at her, the more he felt as if he knew her on some level, that she wasn't a stranger to him.

"I know you," he said, his voice low, his breathing harsh.

She shook her head. "We've never met."

Her voice was sultry, only adding to her appeal. Not that she required any help.

Thor watched her. "No. I know you. I've thought of you before when I'm——" He stopped, realizing he was about to confess to masturbating while fantasizing about her. He didn't date, but he had enough sense to know that telling her he whacked off while thinking about someone identical to her would probably be unwise.

"Thought of me when you were what?" she asked, staying close to him.

He didn't need to see his face to know it had reddened. Swallowing hard, he glanced away. "I've seen you in my head before. Like dreaming while awake."

A slight smile tugged at her full lips. She slid her hand down his arm and lifted his own, turning his palm up. She ran her fingers over the lines on his palm, her smile becoming full-blown. She managed to be even more beautiful. Suddenly, her brow creased. "Your lifeline ends, but starts again. You've crossed over."

"Crossed over?" he asked, barely able to get words out as his mind was a jumbled mess of hormones. He wanted to lift the woman and ravish her. Couldn't she see he was barely holding on to his control?

"You've died and been brought back," she said, continuing to stare at his hand as if it held all the answers in the world. "But you weren't the same when you returned. You were more in some ways, less in others. You wage a war internally, each day you exist, and you're afraid soon you'll lose yourself to it all."

His breathing increased as she spoke of things she should have no knowledge. Yes, he'd been reborn part vampire, but he didn't know anything more about his past than the fact he'd always been able to shift into a panther. It felt too natural shifting forms for it to be anything but what he'd been before.

She closed her eyes and tipped her head back, swaying slightly, his hand still in hers. "There is a darkness that eats away at you. You fear it. And a hunger you think will never be satisfied."

Thor jerked his hand out of hers, wondering how it was she knew so much about him when he knew next to nothing about himself.

She looked up at him. "Lance."

"W-what?" he questioned, as the name that haunted his dreams came from her lips.

"Lance," she repeated, easing closer to him, her body pressed to his.

Thor stepped back quickly as his demon side tried to rear its ugly head. It wanted to lash out and protect him. He would not permit it to harm her.

She stepped closer to him, as if she didn't have a care in the world and he wasn't deadly.

Was the woman insane?

"I'm scaring you," she said before easing back, a forlorn look spreading over her face. "I'm sorry, Lance. I didn't mean to read you. It doesn't happen with everyone I touch."

Thor shook his head, lifting a hand to keep her at bay, more for her own safety than anything else. "Why is it you call me Lance?"

"Because it's *your* name," she said, watching him closely. "Don't tell me you're one of those guys who comes to New Orleans and drinks to the point they forget their own name. Come on, I'll help you get a car back to your hotel. You can sleep it off there. Thank you for your help with Austin and for, uh, offering to kill him and his buddy. That was sweet in a creepy, don't-really-do-it kind of way."

"I've had nothing to drink," he said, his gaze snapping to her neck. He licked his upper row of teeth, his fangs wanting to distend and sample her. Deep down, he knew she'd taste heavenly. That one small bite would never be enough. And while he'd stayed away from the women willing to feed his vampire side at Pierre's home, the idea disgusting him, the thought of drinking from Emi turned him on in ways it shouldn't. It made him rock-hard.

She stared blankly up at him. "But you don't know your name is Lance?"

He opened his mouth, his intent to lie to her and then make a quick exit. That wasn't what happened. "My name is Thor."

She snorted. "As in the god of thunder?"

He nodded.

She grinned. "Well, I can see why you'd get the nickname. You're what I'd think of if I was picturing the Norse god of thunder."

He boldly stepped closer to her. "What did those men want with you?"

"They're ex-friends of a close friend of mine," she said, being as clear as mud in her explanation.

144

"They think I talked him into going home. I didn't, but I'm happy he went. They're no good. He's got a shot at a good life, but they don't."

"Are you the reason there was a wall of power up that stopped them from getting to you?" he asked, remembering how the power had burned him for the briefest of moments.

"Yes." She glanced around nervously.

Thor didn't like seeing her unease. He reached out and took her hands in his, drawing her closer to him. "Good."

"Good?" she echoed. "You're not totally freaked out?"

He snickered. "No. Not at all."

"But you were when I told you your name— which, by the way, is not Thor," she said, shaking her head. "Lance, you're a really strange guy. I like that a lot. Want to come home with me?"

He blinked in surprise. "I'm sorry, what?"

She grinned. "I just tried to convince you to come home with me for the night. The look on your face says that did freak you out."

"You want to take me home with you? Why?" he asked, stunned.

She lifted a brow. "Well, aside from the obvious, which is, you're drop-dead gorgeous, every dead person around you right now is telling me to keep you close to me."

His gaze darted around. She could see the dead? And there were dead people near him?

She laughed. "Relax, they're harmless and very interested in you. Kind of like a moth to flame. I'd judge them, but really, I kind of get it."

Thor wasn't sure how he felt about that. He did know that she wasn't the mission, and a detour could prove fatal. If Pierre found out he'd dismissed his objective to go home with a woman for the night, he'd have Emi hunted and killed. The idea of causing her harm made his body tense.

He knew he should leave her and put distance between them, but he couldn't seem to pull himself away. He didn't want to leave her. He wanted to do the opposite. He wanted to lift her and ram his cock deep inside her and pound into her until they both orgasmed. He wanted to claim the woman with both sex and by sinking his teeth into her tender flesh.

Whoa? Claim?

The idea should have been like ice water getting dumped over his head. It wasn't.

Without thought, he touched her cheek, and then did something that stunned him—he dipped his head and pressed his lips to hers.

When she melted against him and parted her lips, he growled, jerking her to him more. He ate at her mouth, the taste of her driving him wild. Their tongues danced around each other erotically, spurring his need onward.

Emi put her arms around his neck, and Thor found himself lifting her, their mouths still connected. Her breasts smashed against his chest, only serving to increase his hunger for her.

When he realized he was about to try to fuck her against the wall, out in public, in the center of Bourbon Street, he stopped their kiss cold. Their tongues remained laced around one another for a moment longer before she stiffened in his arms.

He set her down gently and broke the kiss. "I'm sorry. I didn't mean to do that."

"You didn't?" she asked, her fingers going to her passion-filled lips, her eyes wide. "It sure felt like you meant it. I was just going for hot dogs. I really didn't expect all this. Not that I'm complaining or anything. This beats hot dogs by a long shot."

She was odd, and he found he liked that about her.

He grinned sheepishly. "Well, I meant it, but I didn't mean to take it so far out here in the open. My apologies."

"Don't take this the wrong way or think I'm easy like those women who were showing off their breasts to anyone willing to throw a set of beads at them, but you could have totally taken that kiss further." She touched her lips more, drawing attention to them.

Thor wanted to kiss her again and test her offer. He resisted if for no other reason than he really would screw her in public, and she deserved better than that. "You're beautiful," he stammered.

She raked her gaze over him. "Ditto."

"I should go now," he said, remaining in place.

She tipped her head. "The spirits around you have made it very clear to me that your place is by my side tonight." She paused, looking at something to his right.

There was nothing there that he could see, yet oddly, he believed that someone or something was there.

"What do you mean, what he's chasing is what has been looking for me?" she asked of the nothingness.

Thor's gut clenched. She couldn't mean Chilton and his secret weapon were hunting her, could she? As he focused on the question, a sinking feeling started deep within him. If she was right, she really did need him by her side. While her magik trick worked to keep away the smelly street men, it wouldn't do anything to stop a powerful vampire.

Emi looked to his left. Her eyes widened. "I'm not telling him that."

"What?" he asked.

"Nothing," she said fast, her upper chest staining with pink.

"Tell me what the spirit said."

She huffed. "How do you know I'm telling the truth about seeing dead people? I could just be crazy, you know."

He smirked. "Call it a hunch, but I don't think you're bat-shit crazy."

"Why aren't you scared of what I can do?" she demanded, looking almost offended that he didn't think she was crazy. Odd woman.

"Sweetheart, I'm the thing that scary things are afraid of," he supplied.

She stared at him, and her gaze eased down him slowly, making his body heat on the way. When her eyes reached his groin, she wet her lips and then jerked back. "Oh, um, yeah. I can see how people would be afraid of you."

Thor chuckled and realized he felt almost normal around her. Like the stress of the world wasn't on his shoulders, as was generally the case. For a moment, he felt less broken.

He was about to draw her into his arms again when the hairs on the back of his neck stood on end. Something dangerous was close, and moving in on their location rapidly.

He knew that scent—Chilton.

Without thought, Thor grabbed Emi's hand and

moved quickly with her through the busy street. She tugged lightly, and he stopped to avoid harming her.

"What's going on?" she asked, her eyes wide as she struggled to keep up with him as he dragged her through the Quarter.

He bent to be eye level with her. "Something bad is coming."

She touched her chest with her free hand and shivered. "The darkness? You sense it too?"

He slid his hand to the back of her head and dragged her against his chest, wanting to not only ease her fear but warm her as well. She should have been hot. It was nearly a hundred degrees, and that wasn't even counting the humidity. Instead, she was ice cold. Worry for her assailed him. "Emi?"

"I'm fine, Lance. But I have to get hot dogs." She trembled in his arms.

He nearly laughed at her train of thought. "Sweetheart, hot dogs can wait. Okay?"

"Okay," she said, her voice barely there as she continued to shake in his arms.

He felt Chilton growing closer, and there was something else with him. A lot of somethings, if Thor's senses were on point. He took Emi's hand in his once more and locked gazes with her, his other hand finding her chin. "Sweetheart, we have to move, now. Are you okay to run? I'll carry you if need be."

"W-what?" she asked, her eyes wide. "Carry me? Why? Wait…run?" She shook, and he held her tighter to him, drawing upon his shifter side to heat his body above normal. She responded to the new warmth and shoved herself against him tighter. As she did, he felt the threat growing near. As much as he wanted to hunt and kill them, his only concern at the moment was the woman in his arms.

The need to protect her was automatic, as if it was encoded into his very DNA. His master's orders meant nothing to him compared to his drive to keep Emi safe from harm. He'd face a hundred master vampires if he had to.

Emi pushed on his chest and stepped back. "It's coming."

"I know," he said, taking her hand in his once again. "We need to run. Can you do that?"

Nodding, she clutched his hand for dear life.

"Follow me, sweetie," he said, turning and moving through the crowds on the street once more. He kept hold of Emi's hand and weaved in and around the seemingly endless bodies. He held back his smile and winked, keeping hold of her as he moved through the Quarter as if he'd been there hundreds of times before. Maybe he had. He couldn't exactly remember much of his life. He spotted a number of rainbow flags dotting the outer edges of a brick bar on the corner above. He headed in that direction, only to have Emi yank on him.

"This way," she said, seeming more alert than before.

Good. He needed her thinking, not in shock. He gave in and let her lead, letting go of her hand, but staying close. He wanted both his hands free so he could either go for his weapon, in a holster in the back of his pants, or let his claws extend. Either would do in a pinch, but he suspected the claws would actually do more damage to another supernatural. Whatever was hot on their trail felt somewhat like a vampire, but more. Though he still smelled Chilton's scent in the mix and it confused him.

And while he couldn't be certain, deep down, he simply knew that what was coming at them wasn't after him, it was after Emi.

There was something else there too, a smell he more than knew.

Beowulf!

No. It couldn't be. Could it?

Chapter Twelve

A MOMENT of sheer panic assailed Thor as visions of Pierre sending one of his pets, possibly Beowulf, to kill Emi came over him. It would be a very Pierre thing to do. Had he orchestrated the moment of male bonding between the men prior to Thor's leaving? Was it all a way to lure Thor into a false sense of security and then gut him when he wasn't expecting it? Sending Thor out to meet someone from his past that he had a connection to, and then having her killed in order to see Thor's reaction, was exactly the type of games Pierre liked to play.

Sick fuck.

One of Pierre's pets could be watching them this very second. They could be reporting back to the master, filling him in on how Thor had rushed to Emi's defense. About how drawn to the woman

Thor was. Worse yet, Pierre could very well be there, watching from a safe distance. It wasn't as if Thor would have sensed him. He'd not even sensed him rise.

I won't let him hurt her.

He had to get her far from the area. Far from the reach of harm. His pulse raced and his thoughts were scattered. Gone was the man who could enter any situation and come out the victor. He'd been replaced by a man Thor didn't know. A man who panicked.

The very idea of Emi being hurt made it hard for Thor to think clearly. All he wanted to do was shift and run through the Quarter in panther form until he hunted and killed every threat there was to her. His beast could track the enemy better than he could. But he had to get her to safety first and then he could do battle. Not before.

He let her lead until the smell of the enemy began to grow to epic proportions. He knew then that the enemy was closing in on them.

Thor twisted, picked up Emi, and began running with inhuman speed. He'd figure out a way to explain it away to her later. For now, they needed to move faster, and he had to get her away from the threat closing in on them at a rapid rate.

He moved swiftly through the streets, going where his gut led him, hoping it was correct. The music from the Quarter grew faint and the horrid smells faded away. Soon, he found himself far from the Quarter and in an area of the city that seemed all but abandoned. There wasn't a soul out on the street. There was a notable absence of light as well. The entire area seemed to be blanketed in darkness. Unnaturally so. It was the kind of darkness and stillness that meant a predator was in the area. Something that scared away everything else—including light.

Fear for Emi struck him hard, nearly making him fall to his knees. He couldn't lose her. He'd only just found her. He steadied himself and then set her on her feet, tucking her quickly behind him, putting his arms out, ready to shift and do battle as he stared around at the darkness engulfing them.

Emi touched his back gently. "Lance?"

"Everything will be all right, sweetie," he said before realizing he'd answered to the name Lance. The more she called him by the name, the more it felt right. Like it was supposed to be so. He didn't have time to think harder about it all. Not with what was happening around them. An attack was imminent. He just didn't know where it would come from or in what form it would arrive in. But he did know it was coming. "Stay behind me, okay? No matter what."

"Uh, anyone else ever tell you that you run

freakishly fast?" she asked, her voice shaky. "And you carried me like I don't weigh a thing. How?"

"I'm sure it's been mentioned once or twice, and I'm stronger than I look." He could feel fear pouring off her. He didn't want her to fear him. Reaching back, he touched her gently. "I'd never hurt you. Please know that."

"Oh, I know that, but what's coming will try to hurt you. I can feel it."

"To get to you, it will have to kill me first, and sweetheart, I'm not exactly easy to kill," he said, staying in front of her.

"How about you not volunteer to die for me? Okay?"

His body tightened in anticipation of what was to come. The air held a threatening note, and Thor caught the faintest hint of a smell he recognized at once as belonging to Chilton. The thick heavy stench of rotting meat took over, and Thor knew instantly what was closing in on them—hybrids.

And not the good kind like he was. The broken, decrepit kind that were mindless killing machines. The defective attempts at supernatural blends. The ones that ended up locked in varying states of transformation when their bodies began to break down as they rejected the additional strands of DNA that had been introduced to them.

Fuck.

They tended to be single-minded and obedient to a point, to those holding their strings, and if what he was smelling was accurate, they were about to be overrun by them.

Turning a slow circle, Thor let his eyes adjust to the darkness, and kept Emi behind him the entire time, wanting to use his body as a shield for her. As he felt the enemy moving in from all sides, he sighed, knowing he was about to become what she feared.

"Emi, please don't freak out at what I'm about to do," he said, as he put his hands out to his sides, his claws emerging quickly.

He had to protect her.

And he had to claim her.

Claim her?

The thought left him unnerved far more than the fact he was about to be outnumbered by zombie-like mutants.

Something snarled, sounding like a wounded animal, a second before a hybrid charged at him from the darkness. It was quickly joined by more.

Thor bent and came up fast as the first neared him. He rammed his clawed hand through the thing's gut, but the action did little to slow it down, as he suspected it would.

Yanking his hand free, he spun, careful to ease Emi out of the way before he slashed out at the hybrid's neck, taking its head from its body.

He expected Emi to scream, run—do anything other than what she did.

She hauled off and punched a hybrid right in the nuts with enough force to make the thing double over.

Once it was bent, she kneed it in what used to be its face, but now that it had two faces, it was hard to tell which was the original. Whatever it had going on, Emi's assault worked to render it immobile for a second.

Thor seized hold of it and clawed its neck open, turning to keep the blood from splattering on Emi.

Emi stared at the thing on the ground and then his hands, her eyes wide. "What are you?"

"I'm like them but not," he said honestly. "I'm a mix of more than one thing, two of which aren't human."

She nodded and drew her lip to one side as if contemplating everything he'd just confided to her. She then pointed at something behind him. "Unleash that not-human stuff on that thing. Eww. And for the record, you are nothing like them. They smell like death. You smell good enough to eat."

Thor took a hit from a hybrid as he realized she was as turned on by him as he was her. Since it wasn't the time or place to fuck her, he pulled his attention back to the matter at hand.

The enemy.

Thor twisted, knocking one hybrid back as more swarmed him. He lost sight of Emi and began to panic, causing him to take blows from the hybrids that he'd have normally been able to block.

Suddenly, someone was there, ripping a hybrid back from him.

A tall man with pale skin, crisp blue eyes, and long brown hair stood there. Thor recognized him as a vampire he'd encountered when on a mission with Belial. He remembered the man being called Auberi. He blinked several times, unsure why the man was there.

Auberi grinned. "Fancy meeting you here, Toov."

Toov?

Thor would have questioned the vampire, but more and more hybrids came rushing at them.

"Whoohoo!" yelled another man as he ran into the fray, his jet-black hair whipping about wildly as he laughed, taking on two hybrids at once. "Good times!"

"Blaise, yer nae right in the head," another man said, who was clearly Scottish, as he sliced through a hybrid. "These things smell like arse."

"And just how often do you sniff ass?" asked

Blaise, strutting on his way to kill more hybrids. The man actually stopped right before he was about to attack two hybrids and started dancing to music only he heard. He spun and did a dance move that coincided with striking a bad guy. He then ran his hands through his hair and rocked his hips, singing something about being sexy and knowing it.

Thor stopped bothering to listen. The jackass was going to get himself killed. In addition to that, Thor had the strongest urge to call someone named Wilson and apologize for ever thinking he was annoying. The problem was, he didn't know anyone named Wilson.

At least he didn't think he did.

"Where are they all coming from?" asked a British male as he joined in the fight. "And did you just say something about passion and pants?"

"Daniel, duck," yelled Blaise, and the British vampire did as instructed. Whoever the men were, they had the situation well in hand, in spite of the fact they'd brought along a jackass.

Thor turned his attention to finding Emi. "Where's the woman?" demanded Thor. His only worry was for Emi. Not himself.

"No clue what you're talking about," said Blaise, still dancing. "There isn't any woman here."

Thor artfully dodged a massive hybrid as it launched itself at him. Twisting around, Thor plunged his clawed hand through the thing's chest and came away with its heart in his hand. There was a momentary delay before the hybrid fell to the ground, its body twitching as it died.

Thor couldn't help but think it a mercy killing.

Living life trapped in a state of mid-transformation while your body rotted slowly, but your mind went fast, was no life at all. These hybrids were different from the ones Pierre called his pets. These hybrids were something else, something that had gone horribly wrong from the get-go. They were the forgotten. The unfortunate souls who were already on borrowed time. Killing them was a kindness.

Another charged him, and he did a double take as he realized it had a body that reminded him of an alligator but its head was partially shifted into something that looked a lot like a rotting bird.

"Oh yuck!" yelled Blaise as he stepped back from a dead hybrid. A long line of what could only be described as snot hung from the man's arm to the body on the ground. "That one gooed me!"

"I fucking hate the gooers," said the Scot.

Auberi moved up alongside Thor, moving fluidly through the enemy. The next Thor knew, he and the vampire were fighting side by side as if they were one unit. Auberi ducked and Thor spun, slashing out above Auberi's head and killing the threat there. Then it was Thor's turn to go low. When he did,

Auberi stood and thrust an arm out, killing another hybrid. The two went on and on, fighting together as if they'd done so on numerous occasions in the past.

"Catch!" yelled the Goth as he threw the head of a hybrid at Auberi.

Auberi batted it away, raised a brow, and then shook his head, cursing in French partially under his breath.

Thor laughed as he kicked one of the hybrids away.

"Laughing only encourages him," said Auberi, a serious expression on his face. "You know how he can get."

Thor didn't know Blaise at all, so he wasn't sure what Auberi was going on about.

Blaise jumped high in the air, and when he came down, he was next to Thor. Grinning, he leaned in close. "Auberi tells me you're family to us now, since Pierre sired you. I gotta say, your new smell is a big improvement on the stench of cat-shifter. Tell me something though, do you ever have the urge to lick your ass or did that go away with the introduction to the vampire side?"

"Hey, taking offense," said a newcomer, his dark hair to his shoulders. He was dragging a dead hybrid with one hand and holding a live one off the ground in the other. "Found these two trying to head to the Quarter."

"Malik has all the fun," said the Scottish vampire.

Thor continued to fight the hybrids as he chanced glances at the men who appeared to be on his side—at least for the moment. They acted as if they all knew him.

Malik killed the other hybrid and then pulled a handkerchief from his pocket and wiped his hands clean. He made quite a production of removing the blood. The moment was short-lived as he twisted quickly, claws emerging from his fingertips as he struck the throat of a hybrid that had tried to get the jump on him. "Their blood is the worst to get out of clothing."

Thor locked gazes with the man and swayed, his mind racing suddenly with images of the guy with much longer hair than he had now. The man was with him, pointing in one direction, communications gear on his head, a weapon in his other hand, dressed head to toe in black. He was issuing tactical commands to Thor. And there was an undeniable level of trust between himself and the man they'd called Malik.

"What the hell?" asked Thor, his attention snapping back to the here and now. He blinked several times, unsure if he'd finally broken mentally.

Malik stared at him. "It's good to see you again, brother."

Brother?

The men certainly didn't look anything alike. Malik's skin was bronzed and his hair was dark, as were his eyes. Thor was about as opposite of that as one could get.

"Amnesia-Boy looks lost," said Blaise. "Bet he's trying to figure out the family dynamic. Tell him your daddy liked to bone Swedish supermodels."

The Scottish vampire laughed. "Would the correct term be memory challenged, nae Amnesia-Boy?"

Amnesia-Boy?

Memory challenged?

Thor concentrated on the men around him, so much so that he didn't notice another hybrid coming at him from the right. It hit him hard, lifting him up and off the ground. The hybrid bit into Thor's shoulder, tearing flesh and muscle, down to the bone. It hurt like hell, but Thor ignored the pain, lifting his hands and sticking his clawed thumbs through the thing's eyes.

He expected it to lurch back from him. It didn't seem the least bit fazed.

Oh shit.

The demon in him wanted to be permitted full freedom. At the same moment, the panther did as well. Thor gave in, knowing the two would blend. He felt his upper body increasing in size and mass. Black fur coated his arms and upper body as his mouth changed shapes.

Snarling, he used the increase in size and strength to thrust the hybrid from him. He then came up fast and propelled himself at the beast. They struck with such a force that the area seemed to shake. He snapped his jaws at the hybrid, catching it by the neck. Its rancid blood filled his mouth and he ripped the flesh back, taking with it important parts before releasing the now-dead hybrid. It fell away and he twisted, spitting the vile, bloody neck tissue onto the ground.

When he turned, he found the other men all staring at him with wide-eyed expressions. The Goth was the first to speak. "Holy fuck, he bit its throat out. That was awesome and gross. Did it taste as bad as it smelled?"

Thor used the back of his hand to wipe the blood from his lips as he nodded. A shaky laugh fell from him when he realized there were no more hybrids attacking them. "Worse."

"Blaise, yer covered in boogers," said the Scot.

Blaise grunted. "And you're an asshole. What's your point, Searc?"

"Toov has hybrid guts all over his face," said Auberi, stepping forward.

Thor lifted a brow. "Why do you keep calling me Toov?"

Daniel stiffened, but then licked his lips and spoke. "Because that is your name."

"Should we be telling him that, Daniel?" asked Blaise. "Can we make his head explode or something? We don't know what my brother did to him when he converted him. Pierre is a total dick with a god complex. He probably figured out a way to put a fail-safe in his mesmerizing-his-minions cocktail."

Malik glanced at Blaise. "Hmm, think stores will start stocking that? Could be all the rage soon. Looking to forget your troubles? One sip cures all your worries."

Blaise grinned. "Warning: Side effects include obeying a total dicknob and getting a stupid god name."

Thor listened closely to their witty banter and then took a small step back. "My name is Toov?"

The men shared a look before they shoved Daniel at Thor, as if they'd designated him the bearer of bad news. The British vampire cast them each a hard look then turned to face Thor fully. "Yes."

"Do you know a man named Lance then, because Emi said I was Lance?" asked Thor.

Blaise slapped his hand over his eyes. "Fuck. His mind is pudding."

"Pudding?" asked Searc.

Blaise shrugged. "I love pudding."

"Yer a douche," said Searc.

Auberi walked toward Thor, filling the gap between them. "Do you remember anything before your time with Pierre?"

"Where is Emi?" Thor demanded, spinning around. She wasn't anywhere to be seen. Had the enemy run off with her?

"Who?" asked Daniel, his voice even, as if he was concerned Thor would snap.

"Woman. Dark long hair. In a skirt. She's beautiful. You can't miss her."

Daniel glanced around. "There's no female among these hybrids and none was here when we arrived."

"She was just here," Thor said, a piece of him wondering if he'd imagined her. "Wasn't she?"

The men shared another look.

"If you say so," said Blaise. "Let's all keep the really strong guy from flipping his lid, okay?"

Auberi sighed. "Enough. I told you before I think he's trying to break the hold Pierre has on him. I think he's fighting to regain his memories of his life before."

Thor shook his head. "Can you help me remember?"

Blaise stepped forward fast and caught Auberi's

arm. "We can't. If we screw with what our brother did to him, we could end up leaving his mind totally broken. You know that. We've both seen it happen before."

Auberi snarled. "Pierre is no brother to us! We may share a maker, but he turned his back on everything and everyone in his quest for power. He is a monster now."

Thor found himself nodding in agreement.

Malik watched him carefully, saying nothing.

Thor pointed to Malik. "I had a quick flash of you. You had longer hair. You were dressed in ops gear and issuing orders to me. Was that real, or are they right about my brain being pudding?"

Malik perked. "We've gone on many missions together. What you're seeing in your head is real. It happened. I can't tell you which mission, because there were a lot, but I can tell you that, yes, we've been together in ops gear on missions. It's been a while, but it happened."

He stared at the men, trying to trigger memories of them, but nothing came. All that did happen was his head started to hurt. A lot. Hot wetness trickled from his nose and he knew it was bleeding again.

Auberi reached out and touched his shoulder. "Don't force yourself to remember. Bad things can happen if you do."

"Worse than not knowing who I really am?

Worse than endless nightmares?" he asked before thinking better of it. "Worse than imagining a woman to the point I thought she was really here with me?"

Auberi didn't look surprised. "Yes. Worse than that. Far worse."

"Yeah, like the kind of bad that leaves someone putting a bib on you, feeding you pudding, and then wiping your drool," said Blaise.

"What the bloody hell is your obsession with pudding?" demanded Daniel.

"Oh, look, the Brit is cursing," added Searc. "Excuse us while we all piss ourselves with laughter."

Daniel grunted. "If you'll recall, I am your team captain."

"So they keep telling me," returned Searc with a salute and a mock grin.

"He gives you hell because you're British," said Malik. "Striker does the same thing to Corbin."

"I'd love to hear Corbin's trick for not killing Striker," said Daniel, sliding a hard glare in Searc's direction.

"Lately he's taken to filling darts with what we call Mercy Juice and shooting Striker in the ass when he's not looking," said Malik. "Boomer too. Duke is worse. He's actually tried to kill them both a few times."

The men laughed, and Thor felt removed from the discussion. Though, he did recognize some names.

Auberi stayed close to him. "Does Pierre have you here in New Orleans for a reason or did you just decide to take a vacation from that asshole and conveniently walk into a hybrid ambush?"

Thor was quiet a second...before he realized that his silence equaled obedience to Pierre. He growled, and then straightened. "He ordered me here to hunt Chilton, and whatever weapon Chilton has."

Auberi's surprise was masked quickly. "Did he forbid you from discussing this with others?"

"He always does that," said Thor.

Auberi looked to Blaise. "Yet he just told us."

Blaise grinned from ear to ear. "Means he's breaking the bond he has to Pierre on his own. Weakening it for sure. Good. Pierre is a bag of dicks."

"So you mentioned," said Thor. "Not that I'm disagreeing or anything."

Auberi laughed. "How about we call in a cleanup crew and then make ourselves presentable before we find a place to discuss what we're all doing here in the city?"

Thor glanced back in the direction he'd last seen Emi—or where he'd last imagined her to be. If she was even real at all. "I want to know more about all of you and how you know me, more about my past. But I swear to you there was a woman here with me. I don't know, maybe I did imagine her. It was so vivid. Dark long hair, dressed kind of like a fortune teller meets flower child, and smelling of sage and lavender?"

"From the dreamy look on yer face, you fancy the lass," said Searc.

Thor inclined his head quickly then cleared his throat. "I don't know what to think anymore. Maybe I'm as broken as the rest of the master's fucking pets."

Malik walked to the edge of the street and bent. He picked up a red piece of material and held it up.

Thor recognized it as the scarf Emi had worn on her head. He gasped and lunged toward Malik. "Emi had that on as a headband!"

Malik sniffed the material and looked to the other men. "It smells like lavender and sage. He wasn't imagining a woman. She was really here, and that means the baddies that got away might have her."

"No!" shouted Thor, nearly losing control then and there.

Blaise grabbed him. "Hold it together, Thor, or whatever the fuck it is you go by now. If you get stuck in shifted hybrid form, you're of no use to anyone, least of all the woman."

Malik nodded and handed the material to each of the men, who took turns smelling it. "Let's split up and look for her."

They nodded.

Auberi and Blaise stood next to Thor. Auberi spoke. "We'll go with Toov."

"Keep him under control," warned Daniel.

"No promises," said Blaise, starting to dance once more.

Chapter Thirteen

EMI THRASHED at the monster that had hold of her arm, its claws digging in deep, drawing blood as it yanked her down yet another side street. It had been doing so for what felt like forever, and while she liked to consider herself an expert on New Orleans, she had no clue where they were.

She struggled to hold her ground and dig her feet in but it didn't work. All it did do was cause the thing's claws to bite deeper into her flesh. Pain raced up her arm, but she ignored it, wanting to get away from the thing dragging her.

"Ouch," she said, jerking harder, to no avail.

It didn't even register she was speaking. When it had first made direct contact with her, ripping off her headscarf, she'd nearly lost control of her gifts as the horrors the thing that had once been human had endured washed over her. She'd seen the testing it had gone through, the tortures it had survived, only to come out the other side grotesque, barely able to register a real thought, and dying a slow death.

It had been too much for her to handle. Too much for her to absorb and compartmentalize as she'd been trained to do. She'd wanted to help it despite the fact it seemed bent on taking her with it, wherever it was going. And it didn't care how heavy handed it was, as noted by the fact it was dangerously close to digging its claws to the bone.

"Stop!" she yelled—and much to her shock, the creature obeyed.

It came to such a grinding halt that she barreled into it and nearly retched from the smell. Unsure why it had stopped, but thankful, she stared up at it. She counted four eyes, none where they should be, and in its mouth, it had double rows of teeth, like a shark. There was no way in hell she was going anywhere else with it. She'd faced demons who were less scary-looking than the thing holding her.

"Let go of me," she said sternly, on the off chance it would listen again.

Much to her delight, it did. It released her.

Weird.

Emi tipped her head and watched it cautiously, curiosity outweighing common sense. Fleeing should have been her first priority, seeking out medical attention her next, but that wasn't what she did. She remained in place, watching the creature as it simply stared down at her. She had to know why it listened to her commands. And would it do it again?

"Hop."

While it did manage to get off the ground, it wasn't so much a hop as it was an entire body leap. When it landed, it did so with a thud. It did it again, and she realized it would keep going until she told it to stop, so she did. For a few seconds, they merely stood there facing one another, each seeming as lost as the other.

Though Emi liked to think she at least smelled better.

She held her injured arm, stopping the blood from flowing as she looked the thing over, doing her best to figure out what it really was. It wasn't a demon. She'd have sensed it. And it no longer human. That much she was sure of. But traces of humanity clung to it like lost remnants.

She sniffed closer, instantly regretting the decision as the smell of rotting meat hit her. The creature mimicked her, sniffing her loudly. It didn't appear as offended by her smell.

That was good.

It pushed at her injured arm and she released it, noticing the cuts weren't as deep as they had been only seconds ago. That was strange.

The creature grabbed hold of her uninjured arm and she nearly yelped, fearful he'd try to rip it off or something. It took her blood-covered hand and wiped it on the tattered remains of its shirt. The gesture was so kind that she almost forgot she was standing face to face with something that looked to have come directly from Frankenstein's laboratory.

"What are you?" she asked.

It didn't respond.

She cleared her throat. "Why did you attack us?"

He stared out at her from all four of its eyes, looking lost as to what she wanted to know. The more she stared at it, the sorrier she felt for the creature. Her injured arm was still too sore to lift, so she reached out and touched the creature with her good hand.

The creature jerked back as if she might hurt it.

Again, she felt pity for the thing. "You weren't always this way, were you?"

It didn't respond verbally, but it did tear up slightly. It was enough for her to know that a tiny portion of the person it used to be was still inside there, trapped. Jolting back, she cupped her mouth, appalled at the idea that the thing before her was still being tortured by being left in the state it was. Who would do such a thing? How was it even possible?

And how could the person behind it all be stopped?

When the creature reached out for her, she half expected it to latch on as it had before and resume dragging her through back streets and alleyways. It didn't. It touched her cheek as gently as it could.

It was then she felt it—the thing before her wanted to die. It wanted to end its existence, and for some reason, it wanted her permission to do so.

"Emi!"

The creature snarled at the sound of Lance's voice as Lance ran around the corner with two men in tow. They looked like a model convention was in town and they'd just fallen off a runway. Each one was strikingly handsome and screaming badass.

Lance's gaze narrowed on the creature next to her and he snarled, putting his hands out like he had previously. And just as before, claws shot out of his fingertips. This time she didn't feel faint, as she had the last time he'd pulled that party trick out of his hat. She'd seen what he could do to the creatures. He could kill them.

She took a stance in front of the creature. "No! Stop!"

Lance drew up short, right before he would have attacked the monster. "Emi?"

She stood in place, lifting her arms, ignoring the pain, trying to block more of the giant thing behind her. She had a feeling she looked a lot like a molehill before a mountain, but still, she had to make an attempt to protect it. Whatever had made it the way it was had done enough damage. It didn't deserve more. "Don't hurt him."

"W-what?" demanded Lance. He tried to grab her injured arm but she moved it away before he could. "He fucking hurt you! I'm going to make his death slow!"

"I don't think he meant to hurt me."

The brown-haired man who had arrived with Lance stared at her as if she were touched in the head. Maybe she was.

"Emi, move," said Lance grimly.

She shook her head. "No. You're not allowed to touch him. He feels bad for hurting me."

"You have got to be kidding me!" snapped Lance. "Hybrids don't feel anything but the urge to kill."

"Hybrids?" she asked.

Lance nodded his head at the thing behind her.

The other man who had arrived with him had jet-black hair with a silver streak in it and enough piercings in his face that he more than likely had issues getting through metal detectors. He tipped his head and lifted his hand as if he intended to whisper to the brown-haired man. "Oh, look. Amnesia-Boy has an insane girlfriend. I'm shocked. Totally shocked. Two crazies. Maybe they'll get together and give birth to Wednesday Addams."

"Blaise," warned the brown-haired man.

Emi looked at the man who appeared to have fallen into a vat of leather. "Oh please, Wednesday Addams would totally be your type of chick."

The Goth guy grinned widely. "Touché."

"Blaise, can you not see how calm the hybrid is being? Have you ever run into one who wasn't snarling and trying to bite your throat out?" asked the brown-haired man, a French accent evident.

"Well, no, but that isn't saying much," returned Blaise with a shrug. "Most people want to bite my throat out after meeting me. Kind of a common response to my awesomeness."

Emi could see how he'd evoke that type of response from most people. She was entertaining inflicting pain on him and she'd only just met him.

Lance made another move to go around her toward the creature. Emi swatted him hard enough to make her hand sting. He froze in place, his gaze narrowing on the creature. "Emi, you need to listen to reason. That thing will kill you the second it gets the chance."

"Yes, but why isn't it killing her?" asked the brown-haired one. "It clearly has the chance, as it's in striking distance, but it is not harming her. Perhaps we should hear her out."

"Auberi, stay out of this," said Lance.

Emi pointed at Lance with her good hand. "Stop trying to bully Frank."

"Who the hell is Frank?" demanded Lance, sounding almost jealous.

Emi bit her lower lip. "The monster needed a name. Since he looks like he's an escapee from Frankenstein's lab, Frank seemed like a great name for him."

Lance groaned. "He's not a puppy. You can't keep him."

She put a hand to her hip. "Who are you to tell me what I can and can't keep?"

Was she really arguing to keep the monster that had nearly torn her arm off? She thought harder on it all.

Yep.

She was. Even she knew that was insane, she couldn't let Frank be harmed any more than he had been. Someone had to stick up for the downtrodden and the monsters of the world.

"Bully him? Frank?" asked Blaise, snorting as he did. "Bully the hybrid. Ohmygod, I'm dying—again —here. Should we call Boomer and see if his sanctuary has room for lab experiments by crazy dicks gone wrong?"

"Sweetie," said Lance, touching his forehead like she was giving him a headache. "Sweetheart, listen to me. That thing doesn't feel anything. It's a mindless killing machine."

She puffed out her chest in an attempt to stand her ground with the alpha males. "It's not totally mindless. And why do you keep calling me 'sweetheart' and saying it in a condescending way? Did you forget my name like you forgot yours?"

Lance smacked his lips together like his patience might be near its breaking point. "*Emi.*"

Blaise snorted. "She is fucking great. Where can I get one?"

"One what?" asked Auberi.

"A sassy little hot chick of my own," said Blaise, pointing to her. "I don't think Amnesia-Boy will want to share."

"Stop calling him that," stressed Emi, her gaze narrowing on Blaise. "And there is no way I'd ever be with you."

"What about him?" asked Blaise, thumbing to Lance.

Emi opened her mouth to say no, but realized she actually very much wanted to be with Lance. She was just annoyed with him at the moment. "Okay, maybe him, but not you. You're a jerk."

"Thanks," he said with a wink. "Now, about Frank. Sorry, but he's got to die. Amnesia—erm—Thor is right. It's totally mindless. It obeys its master to a point and then it's just a feral animal."

"Try to come near him. I dare you," she said sternly. "He has some feelings. Small but there. And he listens to more than his master, or whatever you said."

The men glanced at each other.

Auberi stepped forward. "Explain."

"Stop encouraging her," said Lance.

Auberi grinned. "You encouraged Blaise, seems only right I should get your woman going."

"His woman?" asked Emi. "I'm sorry, but what?"

Lance motioned to her. "We're focused on the killer monster behind you right now. Yell about being *mine* later."

"Start of a claim if I ever heard one," added Blaise, once again pretending but failing to whisper.

"I'm considering killing you," said Lance.

Auberi gave Blaise a shove in Lance's direction. "Here. Make it quick. I'm sick of hearing him yap."

"Eat me," said Blaise, waggling his brows.

Emi suddenly felt like the only adult in the group. "Boys?"

"Boys?" echoed Auberi, reaching down and blatantly adjusting himself through his expensive pants. "I'm all man."

Blaise leapt between the other two a second before Lance tried to attack Auberi. Snarling, Lance lunged for the man again. "She's mine!"

Emi made the sign of a "T" with her hands and whistled. "Time out! Everybody take two steps back from each other, and then you, Mr. Thinks He's a god, have got some explaining to do."

The creature stepped back twice.

Auberi noticed, and gasped. "Blaise?"

Blaise nodded. "Yeah, I saw."

Lance glanced at the men. "Saw what?"

Auberi eyed Emi. "Issue an order again."

She drew a blank.

Sighing, Auberi gave her a look that said he thought she was simple. "Tell it to sit."

"You tell him to sit," she snapped back,

Auberi looked past her at the creature. "Sit."

The creature made a move to attack the man and Emi spun and faced him. "No!"

He stopped at once. Fearful that the others

would try to hurt him, she did as Auberi had first asked. "Sit down."

The creature sat.

"Well, fuck me sideways," said Blaise, letting out a long breath. "Doesn't that just leave more questions than answers. Your girlfriend is a fucking hybrid whisperer. Cool."

"Do shut up," said Auberi.

Blaise put his thumbs through the loops of his black leather pants, drawing attention to his silver belt buckle. It was a pentagram. "Make me."

"Your friends are very mature," said Emi to Lance.

Lance shook his head. "Not really. Blaise has been this way all the years I've known him."

Blaise's eyebrows shot up. "Did Amnesia-Boy just admit to knowing me for years?"

Lance jerked and then smiled wide. "What? No. Wait. Yes!"

Blaise grinned. "Our brother's hold on you is breaking more."

"Stop calling him our brother," stressed Auberi. "We share a maker. Nothing more."

A maker? Emi wasn't sure what he meant by that.

"Really? Then you don't consider me a brother?" asked Blaise, a knowing look on his face.

Groaning, Auberi rolled his eyes. "Bite me,

asshole. You know that isn't the same," he said, the comment seeming at war with his manner of dress and the way he carried himself. He was dressed like he was high-end and fancy, but his words were lowbrow. What a strange mix.

"You wish I'd bite you," said Blaise. "I know better than to take you up on the offer. You'd like it too much."

Auberi shrugged as if the other man wasn't wrong.

Blaise glanced at Lance, who was staring at Emi blankly. Blaise lifted a hand and waved it in front of the blond man's face. "Earth to the memory challenged, you in there or this a pudding thing?"

"Stop with the pudding already, would you?" Groaning, Auberi rubbed the bridge of his nose in a manner that said Blaise made him very tired. It was easy to see the man had that effect on people. "Want me to kill him, Toov?"

Blaise grunted. "Too late. Someone else beat you to killing me by like six hundred years, slow poke."

Emi tensed at the man's words. Surely, he wasn't serious. Was he?

Something deep down said he was.

Blaise kept waving his hand in front of Lance's face like he was trying to snap the man out of a trance. "Uh, Thor, you in there?"

"His name is Lance," said Emi sternly, though she wasn't sure why it mattered so much to her.

"We know that—but, how do you?" asked Blaise.

Auberi swatted Blaise's hand down and touched Thor's shoulder. "You okay?"

"I smelled Chilton tonight. More than once," said Lance, still watching her. "At least I thought I did."

"We could sense power that was similar to his in the area," said Auberi. "We followed it, and that was where we found you being attacked by the hybrids."

Nodding, Lance kept watching Emi, his brows knitting together. "Right before the attack, I actually caught his scent. But before that, I was catching something that reminded me slightly of him, but not."

"Yeah, his mind is pudding," said Blaise, shaking his head.

Auberi sighed long and loud. "You make me tired."

"I make a lot of people tired," Blaise fired back. "I'm just waiting for Thor-Toov-Lance here to make a fucking point. We're immortal, and we'll die before he gets it out."

"Immortal?" asked Emi, stunned.

The creature on the ground made a gargling

noise—and she sensed it then, the darkness rolling over the area, searching for something as it always did.

She drew her inner wards up and reached out, putting her hand on the creature's shoulder to shield it from the darkness too.

Chapter Fourteen

THOR SENSED dark power and reacted quickly, going right for Emi to protect her. She grabbed the hybrid and held it, magik rising around her, reminding him of the wall of power he'd passed through to stop Austin. He knew then for sure that magik was Emi's. It was hard to hide his elation. Seeing the dead was something some humans could do. That didn't make those humans mating material. They needed something else—something more.

Emi had it.

I can claim her.

He stiffened, less surprised by the urge to take her and make her his, and more shocked by the fact he knew something of mating. It wasn't as if Pierre ever spoke on the subject. The master vampire detested the very idea of mating. He thought it beneath him and his pets.

Lance kept his body close to Emi's, his gaze finding Auberi and Blaise as they turned in a slow circle, looking around as if they too sensed the dark power sweeping over the area.

"Chilton?" asked Blaise to Auberi.

"Feels like him," said Auberi, his brows meeting. "But he wasn't this powerful the last time we ran into him. It's been what? Twenty years?"

Blaise rubbed his chin and then nodded. "Yeah, about that. But that's his power. I'd stake my life on it."

"I'd stake you for fun, so don't tempt me," said Auberi.

Thor wrapped himself around Emi, noting instantly that she was cold like she'd been before, when the darkness had scanned the area on Bourbon Street. Whatever the power was, and whoever was doing it, it was affecting her differently than it was the rest of them. He rubbed her arms and kept himself pressed against her, using his body heat to warm her.

She shivered and held one hand on the damn hybrid that she was treating like it was a puppy. Once the darkness passed, Emi released the hybrid and turned into Thor's embrace, permitting him to hold her as he wanted to.

He kissed the top of her head. "You're ice cold."

"I know."

"Does that happen every time that shit comes around?" he asked, concerned for her, and the toll the energy was taking on her.

Her teeth chattered as she nodded.

Frank stood and put his hand on Emi's shoulder. Thor's jaw twitched as the urge to chop off the thing's arm took root.

Emi closed her eyes a moment and then gasped, cupping Thor's face. "Frank knows you. He showed me pictures in my head from his past. You're there, dressed in military gear with other men, training or something. And then he showed me labs."

Auberi moved toward them quickly. "There is no way this creature was created during the Immortal Ops Program with Toov and the others."

Thor froze at Auberi's words. He used to be an I-Op?

"I was an Op?"

Auberi inclined his head.

Thor stilled. "Team One or Team Two?"

Confusion knit Auberi's brow. "What do you mean by one or two? There is only one team."

"No. There are two. I've shadowed Team Two several times, gathering intel and reporting back to Pierre."

Auberi shook his head. "There's been some intel

coming in on our end, claiming a second full team of I-Ops was not only successfully created, but put into field action as well, but we've had nothing to back that claim up."

The pain he felt each time he woke from his reoccurring nightmare slammed through his chest, causing him to step back from Emi and grab himself. He swayed, the pain more intense than he'd ever felt before. His vision blurred, and for a moment he was no longer in New Orleans, he was in a big fancy house, and there were others there. A woman with auburn hair.

He had to protect her. She was important to someone who meant the world to him, but who?

Lukian.

The name hit him like a ton of bricks, making him stagger backward as more images from his past assailed him at once. He saw it then —the man with a weapon aimed at the woman. She'd never survive what he was about to do to her.

The ultimate betrayal—killing the mate of a man who once considered you a brother.

Thor couldn't let that happen. He couldn't allow Lukian to know happiness only to have it ripped away. Without thought or regard for himself, Thor had thrown himself in the path of the onslaught of bullets, taking each one and then twisting, keeping his body in the path and the woman safely out of harm's way.

The bullets had kept coming, riddling him full of holes.

More than he would ever be able to heal from.

And then darkness had swept over him, but he'd felt nothing but peace at the time. No regret.

"Amnesia-Boy!" shouted Blaise.

Thor blinked and found himself flat on his back on the street with Blaise there, bent over him, the man's long hair falling into Thor's face. "What the hell was that? Some kind of interpretive dance? You started jerking all over the place and then dropped to the ground."

Emi was there next to him, her eyes filled with unshed tears, her hands on his upper arm. Her lips trembled as she locked gazes with him. "You remember it, don't you? You remember when you crossed over the threshold to death."

"Yeah," he said.

"That blows," said Blaise. "Now get up. There is a high likelihood someone pissed on that street. If not them, the horses that pull the carriage things."

"Mules," corrected Auberi.

"Your knowledge of the difference is kind of freaky." Blaise grunted. "Remember that time I found you in the stables behind that French brothel? What were you really doing in there?"

"Do shut up," said Auberi.

"I'm with Frenchie there," said Thor, rubbing his chest, chasing away phantom pains.

Thor laid there a moment and then swatted at Blaise as the man reached down to tickle the tip of his nose.

"Who's a good little op boy? That's right, you," said Blaise in a voice one would use to talk to a baby.

Thor snarled, allowing his fangs to distend.

Blaise drew back slightly. "I'm impressed. Didn't know they came in that size."

Thor permitted his mouth to return to normal and smiled. "What you're saying is, mine is bigger?"

"One way to find out," said Blaise, going for his belt buckle.

"I will rip off anything that you whip out," warned Thor, meaning every word of it.

"As will I," said Auberi.

"Your dick was in my face earlier," said Blaise, before groaning and turning red. "I didn't mean it that way. I just meant he was naked in his hotel room and I came in and flopped on the bed and he was standing there, in all his naked glory, and, well —shit—my explanation isn't helping any."

Thor looked between the men. "I had no idea you were a couple."

"We're not," they said together, and loudly.

Blaise appeared offended at how quickly Auberi denied him. He shot Auberi a nasty look. "I like to think I'm your type."

"Think again," said Auberi with a grin. His attention went to Emi, and he licked his lower lip seductively. "She is most certainly my type."

"Careful, the guy formerly known as Amnesia-Boy bites, and I saw what he's packing. I'd avoid fucking with him or his woman." Blaise tapped Thor's head and then stood fully.

Thor laughed and sat up slowly, his body still sore.

Emi stayed close to him, looking like she might burst into tears at any moment. He touched her cheek and was about to tell her that he was fine, when she leaned and pressed her lips to his, silencing him with a passionate kiss. Her tongue found his, and she climbed partially onto him, kissing him with so much wanton abandonment that he forgot where they were and growled, eating her mouth, his hands roaming over her upper body.

There were too many articles of clothing between them. He was about to fix that issue when someone tapped on his shoulder, drawing him out of the moment. He glanced up to find Blaise there, giving him a hard look. He motioned his head to

Auberi. "Really want to take your woman's clothes off in front of him? He's already picturing her naked."

Emi touched her swollen lower lip. "I'm not his woman."

"Yes, you are," said Thor.

Her lips set a thin line before she spoke. "No. I'm not."

"Yes. You. Are." He pushed to his feet and then bent, lifting her gently. He smoothed down her skirt and made sure she was fully covered from Auberi's prying eyes.

Emi gave him a tiny shove. "Stop talking about me like I'm property."

His temper flared, and he found himself standing tall, glaring down at her. He'd never hurt her, but the shifter in him wanted her to be very aware he was in charge. "You're my mate. I've waited all my life for you, and now that you're here with me, I'm not letting you go or out of my sight, so suck it up, buttercup, because you're *so* fucking mine."

Auberi and Blaise drew in huge breaths and stepped back.

"Dude, did he just say outright that she's his mate?" demanded Blaise, sounding more like he was about to take up surfing in place of devil worship, or whatever the hell it was he did in all that black leather.

A small grin touched Auberi's lips, and his blue gaze found Thor. "I believe he did."

"Buttercup? Yours? Tell me, did you happen to buy any drugs for sale on these streets?" asked Emi, her gaze narrowing on him. The harder she stared at him, the less alpha he felt. His panther retreated quickly, tucking tail and hiding from the woman's blistering stare. "I'm only asking because whatever you're on must be some good stuff if you think for a minute that macho line of crap is going to fly with me."

Shit.

"I really like her," said Blaise. "I'd like to put in an order for a feisty woman."

Frank grunted.

Thor looked at the hybrid and thought about what Emi had said. The thing knew him from his past, when he'd been an I-Op. While he couldn't remember much of his time then, he knew in his gut that any man he'd served with wouldn't want to exist as the thing before him.

Emi grabbed his hand. "No, you don't."

"Don't what?" he asked, attempting to play innocent, though he was fairly sure his mate could read his damn mind.

My mate.

He liked the sound of that.

"Someone want to fill me in?" asked Blaise.

"He wants to kill Frank because he feels bad for him," said Emi.

Thor tipped his head, curious if she really could read his mind or if he was simply that transparent. If so, Pierre was a shit signal reader.

At the thought of his master, Thor stiffened. His gaze snapped to his mate. While she had yet to realize how important she was to him, he knew. And he knew he couldn't protect her from Pierre and live. If he killed Pierre, he'd die too. He was blood bound to him, and without ingesting his blood, he'd perish.

He knew on a primal level that if he did as instinct demanded and claimed Emi for himself when he killed Pierre, he'd die and Emi would suffer.

"We should handle Frankie there and then regroup with the others at the hotel," said Blaise.

Auberi withdrew his cell phone and placed a call. "Malik, we have the girl. Yes. All is well. We have a situation to attend to first, and then we will meet you back at the hotel before sunrise."

Emi rushed to stand in front of Frank. "He's not a *situation*. You can't just handle him."

"Sweetheart," said Thor, hating seeing her upset and knowing he was part of the cause of it. "We can't let him live this way. Look at him. He's rotting. He's dying a slow death, and soon there won't be anything left of him mentally."

"I don't care. And I don't care that it's what he wants. It's not right! He's not a threat. I understand about the others. They were killers. Frank isn't. Don't hurt him."

Auberi moved in close to Emi. "You are young and idealistic. It is a good quality to have. Never lose it…but in this instance, you are wrong. We cannot permit a fellow brother to remain this way. We'd demand better of our brethren, should it be us. It is only right we give him the peace he desperately seeks."

She shook her head, tearing up more.

Auberi touched her cheek, coming away with a tear. "Look away, and let us do what must be done."

"No," she whispered, her shoulders slumping slightly.

"Go to your Thor, permit him to ease the pain," said Auberi, something off in his voice. "I will do what must be done."

Emi kicked Auberi in the shin and, to Thor's shock, the vampire looked as if it hurt. "Stop calling my man *Thor*. His name is Lance!"

Grunting, Auberi bent and rubbed the spot where she'd kicked him. "You have fire in you. That's good. You'll need it to help Thor find his way back to Lance fully. Now that you are indeed agreeing he's your man."

Emi looked like she was about to kick him again. Feeling bad for the vampire, Thor rushed in and lifted his woman, carrying her a distance from Auberi. "It's okay, sweetie. I don't mind being called Thor."

That wasn't entirely true.

The name made him think of Pierre.

But Lance didn't feel right yet, either.

The look on Emi's face said she was going to cry. He couldn't have that. Dipping his head, he captured her lips with his.

Instantly, she eased in his arms, letting him explore her mouth. His cock responded in kind, wanting to find solace in her. Now wasn't the time or the place. Reluctantly, he drew back, staying close to her. "I need to get you out of New Orleans and somewhere safe. Somewhere Pierre can't find you."

"We can help," said Auberi. "We'll get you both out of here and far from him."

Thor didn't argue with them, there was no point in it. He couldn't go with them, but Emi could. "I'll take Emi to pack her things and then I'll bring her to you."

"What?" demanded Emi. "I'm not leaving the city. This is *my* city. This Pierre guy can just try to make me go. He's gonna have to get in line behind that Chilton guy you were all talking about. Hell, there's apparently a long list of people after me, so really, what's one more?"

Blaise snorted. "I like her. She knows Pierre is a blowhard."

"Who can kill her with ease," said Auberi, looking at Thor. "Gather what she wishes to leave with and then meet us at the hotel we're staying at." He gave the hotel's name and reached out for Frank. "We can handle this matter."

Frank reached for Emi, and Thor prepared himself to argue more with her. She went to the creature, stepped in close and then hugged it. When she drew back, she was nodding and crying fully. "I know it's what you want. I just wish we could do something to fix you."

Thor sighed. Krauss was behind Frank's creation, and there was no going back from what that mad scientist had done. No fixing it. The man played God but was truly the devil.

Emi's face scrunched, and she eased back from the hybrid. "I understand."

"Total hybrid whisperer," said Blaise, partially under his breath. "Think she can talk to my house-plants? They keep dying."

Auberi appeared unamused. "Because they require sunlight. Something you avoid."

"Oh," Blaise replied, nodding and then walking to the other side of the hybrid. "Time to follow us."

Emi sobbed. "I'm sorry."

Frank bent and patted her shoulder in an awkward manner. He then faced Auberi fully. One second he was calm and huggy, and the next he lunged at Auberi, rows of teeth flashing, spittle flying.

Auberi reacted and killed the hybrid quickly—much faster than he'd dispatched the others.

Emi screamed, and Thor caught her, pulling her back. She shook her head and Thor pressed his lips to her ear. "Shh, sweetheart, Frank attacked Auberi knowing that Auberi's instincts would be to protect himself. Frank wanted to die."

"I know," she said, going limp in his arms. "I want to go home."

"I'll take you home," he said, knowing she wasn't up to hearing that he planned to pack her things and leave with her.

Blaise and Auberi stood side by side, blocking Emi's view of Frank's body on the ground. Auberi called for a cleanup crew and then pulled a hand-kerchief from his back pocket. He wiped away what was left of Frank from his hand. From the look in his eyes, he regretted having to take the kill in front of Emi.

Thor nodded to him, appreciating what he'd done for the hybrid and that he hadn't left Thor to take the kill shot. Emi wouldn't have forgiven him.

Chapter Fifteen

EMI SAT in a refurbished kitchen chair that she and Taylor had salvaged on one of their trash day hunting expeditions. They'd then spent an afternoon painting the table and chairs and recovering the ripped vinyl seat covers. It had been fun and had left them laughing—a happy moment.

Unlike now.

She was just thankful Taylor was long gone. If he could see her now, he'd cause a scene, and he'd likely get himself killed in the process. How had everything gotten turned upside down in her life so suddenly? She'd been on her way to get dinner for Hector and Cherry, and then her world had flipped on its head. Just like it had when she was little.

As much as she didn't want to admit it out loud, Emi knew the time to leave New Orleans had come.

The boogieman had found her. She'd stayed too long in one place like she'd been trained not to do.

And then there was Frank.

Poor Frank.

She hiccupped and nearly started to cry again as she thought of the creature who had once been a man. Someone evil had done that to him. That person needed to pay. They couldn't be allowed to continue.

It had taken Lance nearly thirty minutes to get her to stop bawling like a baby when they'd first entered her house. And he was currently doing his best to avoid any sudden movements, as if that might set her off again. He placed a cup of chicory coffee in front of her. He'd made a phone call, and she wasn't sure how much he'd paid the person on the other end, but by the time he was done, the restaurant suddenly offered delivery of food and coffee.

He eased the coffee closer to her. "Drink."

He'd been so incredibly sweet, and he'd not said a word about the way she lived, though she could tell it bothered him greatly. He'd been unable to mask his look of shock when she'd confessed she didn't have a refrigerator, or lights that weren't running from extension cords, illegally hooked up to the building next door. Basically, she didn't have much of anything.

Cocking his head to one side, Lance looked far off for a moment before standing quickly. "Stay here. Don't move."

She caught his wrist as he stood to his full height, his long hair falling partially free from the tie. "What is it?"

"I hear water running upstairs," he said, his gaze fixed on the ceiling. "Stay here. I'll go check it out."

A half laugh came from her as she kept hold of his hand. "Stand down there, big guy. That's just Fredrick. He's drawing me a bath. It's what he does when he realizes I've had a long day or night."

"Fredrick? You have a man here?" he asked. There was no masking the jealousy in his voice. "And he's getting a bath ready for you?"

His reaction was just what she needed to help pull her partway out of her funk. Lance was jealous over a ghost who, when living, had been old enough to be her grandfather. "Yes. I do have a man up there drawing a bath for me. He's been dearly departed for a very long time, so you can relax and can the jealous-lover bit. Well, that's if jealousy is what I'm sensing from you."

Lance took her hand in his and lifted it to his lips. He kissed the back of it. "Yes. That is what you're sensing from me. Sorry. I don't like the idea of you being with other men."

"What about you and other women?" she asked, instantly regretting the question. "I'm sure you have a long line of women behind you. Right?"

He lowered his gaze. "Maybe. Probably. I don't really know. They aren't important here. Only you are. You're mine."

"You do know we're not a couple, right?" she asked, unsure if she believed her own words. She'd only just met him, but already she knew she didn't want to be separated from him. And she knew that soon enough, they'd join, and it would be out of this world. "And I'm not yours."

"Yes. You are." He kissed her hand again, and she nearly melted. Thankful she was already sitting down, Emi squirmed in her seat, causing Lance to grin cunningly. She couldn't think about anything other than how tempting his lips looked. She already knew what he tasted like—vanilla.

And she loved vanilla.

"Tell me about the ghosts you see," he said, easing into the chair next to hers. He kept her hand in his. "Have you always been able to see them?"

She nodded. "I didn't use to be able to tell them apart from the living. My uncle taught me how to spot and feel the differences. He helped me learn to control that gift, and several others he shared, too. I guess our family could always do it."

"He sounds like he loves you," said Lance.

She pressed a half smile to her face. "He did. He was like an uncle, a father, and an older brother all wrapped into one. He raised me after my parents died when I was little."

"Where is he now?" asked Lance, his blue gaze looking through her.

"He's dead. That darkness you felt tonight, that thing that sent those creatures after us—it killed him."

He frowned. "I'm sorry to hear that. Do you still see him? His spirit?"

She shook her head. "I thought I would, but I've never seen him. Not for lack of trying, either."

"I'm sorry," he repeated, and she knew he meant it. "And I'm sorry about tonight, sweetheart."

"I know," she said, sitting up and leaning toward him. "It's not your fault. Thank you for protecting me."

He drew her against his powerful frame and held her to him as they sat. "When you're ready, we need to pack what you want, and we need to leave. Before sunrise, if possible."

Emi tensed, thinking about the way he'd changed during the attack. "W-what are you? And don't say you're like Frank was, because you're not."

He ran his hand through the back of her hair and held her to him. "I can shift into a panther—fully. And I'm part vampire. When I want, I can be both. So if you break it down, Frank and I are the same, but his body rejected what was done to him. Mine didn't."

She closed her eyes and fought against her mind's urge to deny his words. She'd already seen the truth of them. And she knew there was more to life than most humans allowed themselves to believe. There were demons. There were ghosts. And now she knew there were other things that roamed the night. Men who could turn into animals. And men who drank blood.

Why the hell not? She was being held by one of them now, and she didn't want him to ever let her go.

"You're not scared of me?" he asked, still running his hand through her hair in a loving manner.

"No. I'm afraid *for* you," she confessed. "The dead who were in the Quarter were drawn to you. They sensed it on you. Death and life."

He sighed. "Were they around Auberi and Blaise, too?"

"No," she said. "When they came, all the spirits I'd been seeing vanished. Why? Are they like you?"

"Not exactly," he said softly. "They're vampires. They don't shift into animals too."

Emi put her hand to Lance's chest. "Vampires, shifters, and hybrids…oh, my!"

He chuckled. "Yeah. It's a lot to take in. I know. You okay with it?"

"I know I shouldn't be because it's crazy, but I've seen so much in my life that I'm open to just about anything," she confessed. She drew in his scent again and found herself snuggling her face against his chest more, nearly climbing onto his lap.

"Good girl," he said, kissing the top of her head. "Lance?"

He tensed at the name but answered, "Yes?"

"Why do I want to touch you so much?"

"My animal magnetism," he said, his voice light.

She laughed. "Seriously."

"Because we're mates," he said matter-of-factly, like she had a clue what that meant. He tugged lightly on her hair, forcing her to look up at him. She did. He kissed the tip of her nose. "That means we were made for one another. That our souls are linked."

She'd heard her uncle hint at such a thing before, but he'd never given it a name. He'd only said that her mother had thought her father was linked to her soul.

Lance cupped her face. "At first the urge to claim you scared the hell out of me. And I tried to deny who you are to me. But you're the one real true thing I know in my life. I know you're my mate. I know we're meant to be together forever. I don't care that you say you've never met me before. I know you—my soul knows you. And it's taking every fucking ounce of me to keep from spreading you out on this table and doing what I want to do to you."

Emi couldn't tear her gaze from his. The man was stunningly handsome, and touching him felt right. It felt like she'd been waiting to make contact with him all her life, and she couldn't imagine going back to existing without him. Maybe he was right. Maybe they were made for one another.

Then again, maybe he'd end up hurt because of her. Because of what was after her. The idea of Lance being harmed because of something she'd brought into his life made her start to cry again.

He offered a lopsided smile. "I tell you that I want to do you on the table and you cry."

She laughed through her tears. "No. I'm game for that. I just don't want anything to happen to you."

He perked, his gaze sliding to the kitchen table and then back to her. He swallowed hard enough for her to see and hear. "Game for that?"

She touched his bottom lip with her thumb. "Lance, from the moment I saw you on Bourbon Street, I've wanted to jump your bones. That isn't in question. What is…is what the hell is after me and why did it send a bunch of Franks to get me?"

"You keep calling me Lance," he said, his voice barely above a whisper. "Why?"

"Because it's your name," she said, tugging lightly on his lip. "And while you're every bit the Norse god, Thor isn't the real you. I think you know that."

He nodded.

"Do you want me to call you Thor? I will."

"No. I like that you call me Lance," he said, his gaze flickering back to the tabletop. She knew what was on his mind. It was on hers too.

Boldly, Emi slipped out of her chair and onto his lap fully. She wrapped her arms around his neck as she did, wanting the warmth he provided. He lifted her so she could straddle him better.

Chapter Sixteen

THOR RAN his hands up her back. "Emi."

She kissed him and he found himself taking hold of her peasant skirt and inching it up her legs. When it was up and over her thighs, he eased his hand between them and paused, waiting for her reaction to his intimate touch.

Emi surprised him by pushing her hands down as she kissed him, going for the button of his jeans. She undid it with an urgency that excited him. Within seconds, she had his cock out and was stroking it, bringing him near the edge of culmination with nothing more than her expert touch.

Her tongue dove around his as she tugged on his cock, easing up on his lap more. He went for her panties and intended to take his time with her, ease them off and explore her. The second his fingers skimmed her moist heat, he lost control and struggled to keep from doing a partial shift.

Growling, he tore her panties, opening her legs wide and giving him access to her body. Thor broke the kiss and stiffened. "I'm sorry."

She released his cock and cupped his face. "I want you in me. Stop apologizing and do me. Make me forget everything for just a bit."

"With fucking pleasure," he said, lining up beneath her, his mouth finding hers once more.

As he pressed into her, he clenched his jaw at the tightness. Dear gods, how was he supposed to keep going and not come then and there? "Emi?"

She bit at his lower lip. "Lance, please."

"Is this your first time?" he asked, wanting to be gentle with her.

She shook her head.

He wasn't sure he believed her. Not with how hard it was to enter her. Sure, he wasn't a small guy, but her body wasn't having any of it. He caught hold of the back of her hair and tugged, forcing her head back as he kissed her neck and then used his free hand to ease one of the straps of her shirt over her shoulder. As he did, he realized Emi wasn't wearing a bra.

Within a few short movements, he had one of her breasts exposed, her dark nipple there for the taking. And take he did.

Thor's animal side came flooding up, wanting to sink its teeth into the tender flesh there before fucking the woman into oblivion. His vampire side was no better, wanting him to sink his fangs into her and taste her blood.

All he wanted to do was fuck her, but he couldn't. Not without hurting her.

He licked her nipple and then eased his mouth over it, sucking on it, teasing it sweetly. She responded, grinding her body on his, causing her core to relax slightly, giving him the chance he needed to ease into her.

He took it, pushing in more, inch by painfully slow inch. He had to bite his inner cheek to focus on anything other than just how good she felt. It was that or come then and there. When he was finally in to the hilt, he had to catch hold of Emi's hips to keep her still. If she dared move more, he'd lose it.

Her dark gaze slid over him as she lowered her head, her lips trailing kisses all over his face. She whimpered, and he released his hold on her, letting her move freely. The little minx began to ride him hard and fast, to the point he threw his hands out to his sides as they partially shifted into panther form.

Suddenly, Thor could hear her heart beating, see her veins pulsing. The temptation to taste her blood was so great, he had to close his eyes tight as she rode him, her body drawing pleasure from him.

All the while, he felt like he was about to jettison seed into her at an alarming rate.

Do not come.

Do not bite her.

Do not claim her.

Fuck.

Oh fuck.

Holy shit, I'm going to come, bite her, and claim her.

Fuck.

Her lips moved over his and he kept his arms out wide, afraid he'd cut her without meaning to. She rode him faster, and he couldn't stop his beast from surging up more, making fur sprout over his arms and his upper chest. His eyes snapped open, and he froze, sure he'd scared her and the pleasure would end.

Emi looked him over, and then she grinned before biting her lower lip. She yanked his shirt over his head and tossed it aside. She ran her hands through the extra hair on his chest and then began to move up and down on him slowly, making figure-eight patterns with her hips as she did.

He was going to die then and there.

She was going to kill him with sex.

And I'll die a happy man.

"Lance," she said, her lips near his. "Touch me."

"I can't," he said, hating his lack of control. "I'll hurt you."

She ran her hands down his arms, but hers weren't long enough to reach his hands. She pulled on his forearms. "Touch me, Lance. You won't hurt me."

Reluctantly, he gave in and brought his clawed hands in more. As he touched her, he instantly found his center of control, and his body returned to normal form. He used the moment to slide his hands up and under her shirt and cup her breasts.

She increased her pace on him. "Mm, you feel so good."

"Sweetheart, I've never, ever felt anything as good as you." He didn't need his memories to know as much.

She went for his mouth again, and he squeezed her breasts as she bounced on his lap, taking his cock deep into her tight body. He felt her coming a second before she cried out and bit his lip hard enough to draw blood.

His darkness reared its ugly head, liking the pain and the blood play.

Emi licked the blood from his lips, and the second she swallowed, it felt as if Thor was slipping out of his body and into her. He blinked, positive he saw himself through her eyes, felt what she felt—

confused, happy, sad, scared, safe, and the stirrings of love.

Exactly the same way he felt about her.

In an instant, he was back in his body again, unsure what had just happened. He was also unable to stop his fangs from distending. As he was about to try to make them to retract, Emi kissed him quickly, thrusting her tongue into his mouth, catching it on one of his fangs.

As her coppery blood spilled onto Thor's tongue, his shifter and vampire sides went nuts.

She tasted even better than he'd imagined.

Mine.

The word beat at him, wanting out.

With a gasp, he was suddenly seeing from her point of view again, feeling her feelings again. Confusion gripped him as he seemed to slam into his own body once more.

Emi cried out again, and her pussy tightened around his cock.

Thor tried to hold on longer but couldn't. With a growl, he came in scalding waves into her. His body tight. "Mine," he said before thinking better of it.

He sucked in a big breath, terrified he'd just laid claim to her.

Had he? She hadn't said it back to him. Didn't

she have to say it too? And they hadn't bitten one another, so they couldn't be mated yet. Right?

Worry gnawed at his gut.

She kissed him, and he stood, staying rooted in her, still coming. He leaned their joined bodies over the kitchen table and swept whatever was on it onto the floor. The coffee mug broke, spilling chicory coffee everywhere.

He didn't care.

All that mattered was being in Emi. With his cock still ready for more, Thor began to pump in and out of his woman, taking his time loving her.

Chapter Seventeen

THOR WITHDREW FROM EMI, instantly missing the feel of her hot, wet sheath wrapped around his cock. He wanted to ram back into her and give in to the baser need to lay claim to her and make her his for all time. He could. She was right there, ready for the taking, her breasts full, her legs spread, her sex near the head of his cock. He watched as their combined juices leaked from her.

Unable to stop himself, Thor rubbed the tip of his dick through it and teased her tight opening.

Slide home. Claim her.

The need pulsed through him.

She ran her hands over his chest, raking her nails on his skin slightly. The action felt good and appealed to his darker side. It liked the temptation of pain with sex, and wanted more.

"Keep that up, and I'll be back in you," he warned, still rubbing the head of his cock against her entrance.

She squirmed and took the tip of his dick into her body. "Promise?"

A low growl came from him as he struggled to keep control of his darkness. "Emi, I can't. I came so close to biting you during sex."

Her eyes widened. "Biting me? Is that because of the vampire in you?"

He nearly laughed at how innocent her question was. "Partly. But the animal in me wants the same thing. They don't often work together, so when they do, it's extra hard for me to stay in control."

"Why do they want to bite me?" she asked, her voice light, her hips still squirming, teasing him.

He left his cock partly in her, wanting to drive deep but holding back. He grit his teeth. "It's how my kind mate. We fuck and we bite. There is blood involved, and then the pair is bonded—for life."

"That sounds hot and scary," she said, raking her nails lightly over his torso once more. "Would it hurt? You biting me?"

"Honestly, I don't know." He stared down at her neck and shoulder, wanting to sink his fangs into her while he drove his body into hers. "I don't think I've ever claimed anyone before."

As he said it, he knew deep down that he hadn't.

That he'd teetered on the edge once before in his life, though he couldn't recall the specifics, but even that hadn't been like this. It hadn't been this call he felt in his bones to make the woman beneath him his forever.

"When you say for life, what does that mean exactly?" she asked, moving her hips just right and driving herself onto his cock more.

He closed his eyes for a fraction of a second to compose himself. "I'm immortal. Claiming you would make your lifespan match mine."

He resisted the urge to explain to her that it would also mean she'd suffer greatly when he died, and possibly perish herself. That was why he couldn't give in and claim her. He was bound to Pierre, and one way or another he had to break that bond, which would result in his death.

He would never let Emi suffer because of that.

"Lance," she said sweetly. "What we did didn't really feel like fucking to me."

He was about to comment that it didn't feel like that to him, either, when another thought occurred to him. "And exactly how would you know the difference? Who have you been with?"

She gave him a cross look and then smiled wide. "More than you. Since I'm sure you've been with more than just me, how about we leave it at that. Unless you want to leave."

He didn't want to pull out of her, and he certainly didn't want to leave her. Damn woman knew just how to make him obey like a whipped puppy. He grunted and then tugged on the top of her shirt, yanking it down to expose her right breast. He bent and took her pert nipple into his mouth, pressing into her pussy more.

Fuck.

She was pure sage-tasting goodness.

He sucked on her nipple and worked himself deeper into her until he was fully settled in her depths. Her body squeezed him to the point he thought he'd pop then and there. Emi ran her hands into his hair and held his head in place as she bucked her hips against his body.

He thrust, and she met him with eager readiness. Once again, the table squeaked as if it might not withstand the carnal activity taking place upon it. He didn't care if they ended up flat on the floor. He wasn't about to stop.

Not when she felt this fucking good.

He lifted his head from her breast and began to pump hard and fast into her, causing the table to shake more and her breasts to bounce. The sight of them, moving with each thrust, only served to turn him on more. Not that he required anything extra.

"Fuck," he growled, wanting to come then and there.

Emi gasped with each pump of his cock into her.

Thor reached down and rubbed his thumb over her swollen clit, drawing moans of excitement from her. He worked the small bud until she cried out, her body tensing as her hot, wet channel tightened around him.

Thor's jaw went slack, his panther and vampire doing their best to seize the moment and claim her. He held them at bay, lifting his hand and pounding so hard into Emi that the table began to move across the kitchen floor. He walked with it, thrusting into his woman.

When he exploded, it was deep inside her, his body releasing all he had to offer. With a shaky breath, he lay on her, his lips finding hers. In that moment, he knew she'd managed to steal his heart in the blink of an eye, and he didn't ever want her to release it. He was falling in love with her.

When the kiss ended, he stayed there above her, knowing what pure joy truly was. He glanced at the spilled cup of coffee on the floor. "Sorry about your coffee."

She snorted. "Worth it."

"I'll have more sent over."

"Lance, you don't have to spoil me. I like being with you for you, not what you can get me."

"Sweetheart, I plan to hand you the world."

And he did. He had a lot of money put away, thanks to Pierre's overindulgences. Thor would see to it all the money went to Emi.

Her hand found the spot they were joined and she cupped his ball sac. "Pretty sure you just gave me the world there, big guy."

He grinned sheepishly.

She touched his chin. "When we were doing our thing, did you happen to experience anything weird?"

"Hmm, let's see. I partially shifted into panther form and then let my vampire fangs out to play. Does that count?" he asked, embarrassed he'd lost control in such a way.

She snorted. "Yes, that was odd, but not bad. I mean, did you feel like we slipped skin for a second and were seeing out of each other's eyes? Or did I imagine that?"

He tensed. "You didn't imagine it."

"What does it mean?" she asked.

He shook his head. "I don't know."

She stared past him at something.

He followed her gaze, expecting to see someone standing there in the doorway to the kitchen. There was no one there. At least not anyone he could see. He strongly suspected there was someone that his mate could see.

Damn ghosts.

Instantly, his urge to carry on with more sex was doused.

"Dead people are looking at my naked ass, aren't they?" he asked, positive a spirit was now standing behind him.

Emi giggled and wrapped her legs tighter around his waist. "Mrs. Pumpernickel says it's a fine backside, indeed. One you should be proud of."

He tensed, and Emi laughed more. With everything he'd seen since becoming one of Pierre's pets, he shouldn't have been put off by the idea of ghosts, but he had to admit it bothered him knowing someone he couldn't see was watching him have sex. Also, he wasn't sure how he felt about ghosts being real. He'd never put a lot of thought into life after death. "Mrs. Pumpernickel? That is quite a mouthful."

Emi stared past him and her cheeks stained pink. "She says, yes, you do look like you're a mouthful."

Thor joined her in blushing. "How long has this Mrs. Pumpernickel been watching us?"

"That she's let me know about?" asked Emi, biting at her lower lip in a tempting manner.

Thor fought the urge to overreact to the idea they'd been spied on by the dead while getting busy. "Yes."

"Just a little bit," said Emi, running her foot

down the back of his leg. She laughed softly as she did. "Freaks ya out, doesn't it?"

"You think this is funny, huh?" He loved seeing her laugh. Loved the way she naturally touched him whenever he was worked up, as if she sensed he needed her calming energy. He loved the way her body responded to his touch. Truth be told, he loved everything about her.

She waggled her brows. "I do."

He nipped playfully at her jaw, the urge to claim her rising in him once again. It took several seconds for him to cage his inner beast and lock his demon side down. They wanted Emi claimed fully. To hell with only getting to make love to her. His shifter and vampire sides wanted to know she was theirs forever.

So did he, but he couldn't.

He resisted. It was difficult. But he managed. "Can you tell Mrs. Pumpernickel to go away now, because I'm not done with you and I'm not really into putting on a show for others?"

"You just told her. She can hear you," she said, and then looked over his shoulder and laughed more. "But Fredrick is watching you now, and he looks like he's torn between attacking you for touching me, and making you state your intentions, now that you've clearly marked your territory here."

Of course, his woman would not only see dead

people, but she'd see ones who wanted to fight with him. "Fredrick is the bath guy?"

She nodded.

"And he wants me to make an honest woman out of you?"

She giggled more. "Yes."

As much as it pained Thor to admit it, he liked the dead guy, even if he'd never met him face to face. The guy clearly cared for Emi and wanted to know she would be taken care of. It was hard to fault that logic.

Thor cleared his throat and looked over his shoulder to the doorway that was empty as far as he could tell. "Fredrick, she's my mate. I'd die before I'd allow harm to come to her. And trust me, if I thought for a second that I could lock it down with her safely, I would. Now, if you'd be so kind, could you go off with that Pumpernickel lady and let me continue making love to my woman?"

He stayed in place and stared down at Emi. She was even more beautiful covered in his love marks, her skin flushed from their passion, and her lips full from being kissed again and again. He wanted to strip her entirely and lick every inch of her glorious body, but not with an audience.

She cackled. "Ohmygod, Fredrick says you better put a ring on my finger now. He's so old school." Her eyes widened a second before she laughed harder. "Mrs. Pumpernickel is back, and she says that with an ass like yours, she'd be fine with me living in sin."

Thor groaned and buried his head in the crook of Emi's neck. His whiskers tickled her, and she laughed, tipping her head, trying to escape. He didn't let her go. He kept her pinned to the table, his body above hers—as it should be.

He grinned down at her, and, for the first time since he'd come to as one of Pierre's pets, he felt true happiness.

Pure joy.

She ran her hands through his hair and then tugged, bringing his lips closer to hers. He smiled against her mouth, his cock twitching back to life, wanting more of her. He stilled.

"Sweetheart, are we alone now?"

"Yes."

Reaching down between them, he took hold of his cock and stroked it, lining up with her wet core. He wasted no time ramming deep into her, making her cry out as he clung to his resolve to keep from instantly coming and biting her.

Chapter Eighteen

THOR CAME awake to the sound of water dripping in the bathroom sink. The steady drops echoed throughout the room. He blinked away the sleep from his eyes and took a moment to realize where he was and who he was with.

Emi.

His woman.

Smiling, he turned to find her asleep next to him, on the bed, wearing nothing but a small black tank top and a matching pair of black panties. He wanted to be in her again. Hell, he never wanted to leave her body. Each time he sank into her depths, he felt heaven—Nirvana.

And he'd found heaven seven times with her. If he was lucky, he'd find it seven more times soon. He'd never get enough of her.

Ever.

As much as he wanted to join with her again, she was out cold and needed her rest. He'd kept her up for hours making love to her. He resisted the urge to slide over her, and instead sat up on the bed and looked around the room. The sun was just setting again, and he knew they were on borrowed time, staying at her home.

He needed to get her to Auberi and the others. They'd see to it that she was taken far from New Orleans and from Pierre. They'd do what he wouldn't be able to do—protect his mate.

The thought of being without her clawed at his gut. He stood slowly, not wanting to wake her. What he really wanted to do was thrash about the room in a temper-tantrum because he knew he had to give up his mate—the woman he was falling in love with.

If he even knew how to love anymore.

He went into the bathroom and looked into the small broken mirror above the old sink. Emi's house was a total shithole. The fact it was where she lived infuriated him. He'd see to it that the PSI guys got enough money to make sure Emi never wanted for a thing long after he was gone. She'd never have to live in a place without electricity of its own, without any form of heat or air conditioning, and with fucking floors that felt like you'd fall through them at any moment.

He stared at his reflection and exhaled. "Go with her."

As the words left his lips, he knew he couldn't. Pierre would never let him leave, and he'd die without Pierre's blood. The only option he had was to go back to his master and kill him. That would mean his death as well, but so be it. It would also mean Emi would never be hunted by the madman.

His death was a small price to pay for that comfort.

He stared harder at himself, and as he did, his mind began to play tricks on him, showing his reflection without the beard and long hair. In the reflection he was clean-shaven, and his hair was cut close—high and tight. There wasn't a stranger there. He knew the man. It was the man he'd once been. The man before the vampire.

Lance.

The harder he stared at the reflection, the more it all began to come flooding back to him. He saw himself as a child. Saw himself losing his parents before enlisting in the military, wanting to serve his country. Wanting to be everything he could be and more.

And he'd certainly gotten more.

A hell of a lot more.

He saw himself going through endless bombardments of tests, all aimed at making him a super soldier. He saw men around him, going through the same things, some doing well, others struggling. Men hooked to machines with wires all over them. Men in tanks of water, looking as if they were desperate for air. Men running, while other men in white lab coats timed them.

The flashes continued, pouring over him, bringing with them memories of a life he thought he'd never know.

One he wasn't sure he wanted to know more about.

He saw a man with amber eyes and blond hair, participating in the tests as well, laughing with Thor. Another man approached, he had shaggy black hair and blue eyes. He said something, and they all laughed, slapping each other on the back.

Thor's chest tightened, but not with pain, as had been the case for so long. It tightened with emotions. He knew these men. They were like family to him.

Additional flashes hit him, and he gasped, grabbing the sides of the sink as he recalled everything in detail that he'd gone through to become a super soldier.

What had left him a shape-shifter.

He'd willingly participated in genetic engineering and DNA manipulation. He'd learned what they'd been up to and he'd stayed in the testing, wanting to do his part. And he had. He'd served his country for decades, no longer aging. And he'd been happy.

He'd been an Immortal Op.

Part of the elite team he'd been taught by Pierre was the enemy.

The same team he'd been told to kill on sight.

They were really his brothers in arms. His family.

They fought against men like Pierre. Against evil. The very things Thor had aligned himself with since he'd come to be under Pierre's thrall.

"Your name is Lance. Not Thor," he said flatly to his reflection that had morphed back into what he looked like now.

"It's really about time you realized that," said Emi, surprising him by being so close. She put her hand on his shoulder, went to her tiptoes and kissed his cheek before swatting his naked backside playfully.

He twisted and lifted her off her feet, kissing her thoroughly.

She pressed on his chest. "Oh no. I can feel you getting hard already. I'm too sore. I need a break."

He flashed a sexy smile. "I could lick all your sore spots. I just so happen to recall my saliva has a healing agent in it."

She pursed her lips. "Handy. Weird and kind of gross, but handy."

He laughed, and then remembered what he had to do. He had to get her over to the PSI guys then hunt down Chilton, handle him, and then go and kill Pierre.

A walk in the fucking park.

He glanced around the bathroom, trying to sense any spirits. He didn't want to put his clothes back on, as they had dried blood on them, but he'd have to soon enough so they could leave.

Emi grinned. "We're alone."

He exhaled and set her on her feet. "Good. Not that I'm against the spirits or anything, it's just, well, it kind of freaks me out."

She snorted. "You're so good at hiding it."

He kissed her quickly. "I'm going to wash up a bit and then we'll need to head out, okay?"

She nodded. "Sounds good. I just need to check to see if Hector or Cherry can keep an eye out for Rocky and take care of him while I'm gone."

"Who's Rocky?"

"My ex-roommate's dog. Kind of. Rocky doesn't really belong to anyone. Still, he needs looking after. Plus, I should probably let Hector know I'm okay. I went off for hotdogs last night and—"

"Emi!" a deep male voice called from the lower level.

Thor went on high alert, ready to attack.

Emi snorted and touched his bare chest. "Speak of the devil. That's Hector. He's probably worried about me. I'll toss on my pants and go down and explain what happened."

Thor lifted a brow. "You're going to tell him you were attacked by hybrids and then brought a half-shifter, half-vampire home with you and had sex with him?"

"You did what?" asked a tall man as he entered the bedroom, his dark gaze ablaze as he stared at the open bathroom door.

Thor thrust Emi behind him and snarled, unconcerned with the fact he was naked.

The man didn't seem to give a shit, either. He pointed at Thor. "If you hurt one hair on her head, I'll ram a paintbrush up your ass so far, you'll be able to watercolor out of your nose."

"Huh?" asked Thor, calming slightly. The man was no threat.

"Hector," said Emi, rushing around Thor toward the man. She put her arms out and hugged him, wearing nothing more than the tank top and panties. "I'm sorry. I should have found a way to tell you what happened."

"Something big went down just outside the Quarter. When you didn't come back, I enlisted everyone's help trying to find you. We couldn't get into the house last night. Try as we might, it was locked down tight."

Emi sighed and looked up at the ceiling. "I think my dark troublemaker was actually trying to be helpful. Go figure."

"Emi," said Thor sternly. "You're not dressed, and stop hugging the man."

She huffed. "You're naked. And trust me, of the two of us, Hector isn't going to notice anything about my body. *Yours*, he'll notice."

Hector grinned and nodded his head to Thor. "I'm faithful to my man. You're safe." He raked his gaze over him slowly. "And now that I know you didn't hurt our Emi, might I say you have the perfect body."

Thor gulped and cupped himself, suddenly self-conscious about being nude. "Um, well, uh...thanks?"

Emi snorted and pushed Hector out of the room. "Taylor probably left clothes behind. I'll see what he has and what might fit you. I'll also convince Hector that he doesn't want to try to shove a paintbrush up your ass."

"Thanks."

Hector looked back at Thor. "You're really a shifter and a vampire?"

"Yes," replied Thor, waiting for the human to scream or faint.

Instead, Hector smiled and touched Emi's cheek. "Good. That means he'll be able to protect you."

"Why aren't you freaking out?" asked Emi.

Hector winked. "I have a few secrets of my own. Now, let's go see what that vagabond Taylor might have left behind that we can dress that spectacular specimen of a man in."

Chapter Nineteen

HECTOR PRACTICALLY SHOVED Emi through the door to Taylor's room. He then shut the old, creaky door tight behind him. It lacked a handle, so it didn't exactly stay shut with any sort of ease. It had been on her list to fix, but she'd never gotten around to it—like the floor, and so many other things in the old home.

Hector pointed at her. "Oh girl, start explaining the naked supernatural hunk in your bedroom, right now. And I'd like to put emphasis on *super* and *hunk*."

"Why aren't you more focused on the fact he's not human?" she questioned, not that she didn't agree that Lance was a super hunk. Seeing him naked had only confirmed that he was the sexiest man alive.

Okay, mostly alive, with the whole part-vampire thing. She still wasn't sure how that worked. All she knew was that she could sense he'd crossed over the threshold of death, and had spent longer there than most who claimed to have had near-death experiences. His hadn't been near. It had been actual and factual. He'd been dead for enough time that his soul had crossed fully, but then had been ripped back. He now walked with one foot in and out of death.

And that was something that attracted the dead to him. They were curious about him. Drawn to him in a similar way that she was, though she knew her pull to him was more intense. Something that she couldn't control and didn't want to bother trying to.

Maybe he'd been right when he'd said they were mates and made for one another. It would explain how she'd been unable to look away from him when she'd first seen him in the Quarter. Why she'd been unable to keep from touching and why she'd given herself to him so quickly, when she'd made the one other person she'd been with in her life wait much longer.

And why she wanted to be with him again.

Always and forever.

Hector was quiet for a moment before taking a

deep breath. "I know that you haven't told me everything you can do, Emi. I realize that seeing and talking with the dead, and being able to read the past and future on the living, is only part of what you can do. I've never pushed you to tell me everything. I've never asked for proof of any of it."

Emi didn't comment. There was nothing to say. While she'd never outright lied to him, she'd omitted things over the years, mainly to keep him safe and from thinking she was a total and utter freak. And he was right. He'd never once made her prove her gifts to him, and he'd never asked for a reading or if she ever saw dead loved ones around him.

She didn't, but he'd never asked. It was like he already knew the answer.

How did one tell others that she was sure she was personally being haunted by what could only be called a boogieman, and that she thought she had similar abilities to the dark thing that hunted her?

The conversation didn't seem to want to roll off the tongue.

Hector put out his hand and stared at it a moment—before a small but bright ball of fire appeared in his palm.

It was mesmerizingly beautiful, and alluring with its rolling movement and mix of yellows, reds, and orange. For a second, the lure of it was so great that she almost reached out to touch it, captivated by its very existence.

As quickly as it started, it stopped.

Gasping, Emi shot forward and grabbed her friend's hand to be sure he wasn't hurt in any way. "Hector!"

He chuckled and gave her a hug. "Nile told me to tell you years ago, but I'm so used to keeping what I can do a secret, the idea of letting anyone else know is foreign to me."

She blinked and checked his hand again for signs of injury. There were none. "What, exactly, did you do?"

"I can create fire. It's not something I advertise. And since I was adopted, there is no telling where I got the gift from. I've just always had it. Kind of like how you've always been special—more than others."

She gulped. He'd hidden something that big from her all these years? "Wow. I had no idea. Here I thought your threat to attack Austin with a paint-brush was empty."

Hector's expression changed. He put his hands on her shoulders. "Emi, about Austin…"

She tensed. When Taylor had told her that he was leaving, she'd expected issues with Austin. For some time, Taylor had been a high earner for Austin and his crew. The absence of Taylor would be felt monetarily by Austin. And there was no way the man would lose money willingly and be okay with it. Flexing his muscles was something he had to do to save face with the rest of the guys he ran with. Had Lance not stepped in when he had, she'd have set Austin in his place herself, teaching him that he wasn't the baddest thing around.

But Lance had thought he was helping. That he was protecting her. While sweet, it meant Austin didn't get handed his due, and he didn't get the justice he was looking for. She should have known that he'd run off too easily after the Bourbon Street confrontation. Of course he'd seek out Hector and cause problems. He'd probably hassled everyone in Jackson Square in an attempt to locate her.

"Oh no. He came by your stand to harass you, didn't he? I'm sorry! So much happened last night that I didn't think to find you."

Hector shook her lightly, his gaze hard. "Emi, focus. Austin won't be harassing anyone ever again."

As the words left his mouth, Emi spotted movement in the back corner of Taylor's bedroom, near the exterior wall and boarded-over window.

When she realized the movement was Austin, she screamed—but it died quickly as her senses told her the truth of the matter. Austin wasn't there in body. Only in spirit.

He no longer walked among the living.

He looked confused and scared.

She couldn't blame him.

"He's dead," she said softly.

Hector nodded, paying no mind to the apparition. She knew he couldn't see Austin.

He turned slightly and put himself in front of Emi. "Austin is here, isn't he?"

"Yes," she said, pointing in the direction where he stood. "What happened to him? Hector, tell me you didn't kill him."

Austin's gaze narrowed. "Hector? The painter dude, kill me? Uh, no."

"I don't like knowing he's in your house, Emi. I didn't trust him when he was alive. I certainly don't trust him now that he's dead. And you're barely dressed," said Hector, still standing before her, but looking too far to the right to where Austin actually was.

Hector was starting to sound a lot like Lance. She didn't need another man bossing her around. Lance was a big enough pain in the butt when it came to alpha displays.

Emi grunted and walked around Hector. "Dead people are my thing, Hector. He can't hurt me now, but I can put a world of hurt on *him* if he pushes me. I can trap his spirit in the closet for eternity. That would totally suck for him."

Putting his hands up, Austin took a step back and fell through the wall. He reappeared, looked behind himself at the wall he'd just basically fallen through, and then stared at Emi with wide eyes. "I swear I'm not here to cause problems. Taylor told me once that you can communicate with the dead. I hoped you'd be able to see me."

She stared at him, her hands going to her hips. "Let me guess, you're one of those dead people who saw the error of their ways as they were dying and really don't want to end up in whatever version of hell you believe in?"

He pursed his lips. "Yes."

She glanced back at Hector. "Good news. Austin is less of a dick dead. Kind of."

Hector appeared surprised. "Does he smell any better?"

Austin ignored him and stared at her, his expression grim. "Emi, I'm here to warn you. Something bad is coming for you."

She nearly laughed. "You're here to warn me? Really? Weren't you trying to attack me just last night?"

His expression fell. "Yes, and trust me when I say, I really regret that. I've seen the light."

She eyed him. "Oh really. So you came to tell me something bad is after me? News flash, I know."

He shook his head. "You don't understand. It knows where you live now. I'm sorry. I didn't mean to tell him. He was torturing me, and he'd already killed the guys with me." He looked down at the floor. "I was weak, and he told me he'd stop hurting me if I told him where you lived. He said you'd managed to somehow block him from sensing where you were most times—and that he couldn't center in on your location or where you live."

Emi watched Austin, realizing how small and frightened he looked, now that he was dead. Gone was the tough-guy routine he'd had for as long as she'd known him. Now he looked younger as well. She almost felt bad for him.

Almost.

"Emi, this guy isn't…he's not human. He's a monster. And he's headed here for you, and for some guy he wants to kill for daring to think he could touch you. My guess, the blond dude you were with."

"Lance?" she squeaked, as concern for Lance hit her hard. "What does this bad guy want with him?"

"I don't know. But right before he killed me, he looked me in the eyes and said I was going to die for thinking I could try to hurt you. And that your new friend would soon learn what happens to anyone who gets too close to you."

She'd known this would happen. Her uncle had always warned her that those close to her would be hurt, and to always stay on the move. She'd foolishly thought she could carve out something close to a life in New Orleans, and that she'd be able to keep it. Now, people were dead because of her, and Lance was in danger. All because she'd been selfish.

Her emotions welled and she lost control of them, breaking down then and there.

Hector grabbed her and pulled her against him. "Emi, what is it?"

"Austin is dead because of me," she said.

"He's dead because he's an asshole," returned Hector, drawing a righteous huff of indignation from Austin.

Emi trembled. "What's been hunting me found him, Hector. It found him and tortured him to extract information about me. When he gave in, it killed him."

Hector's entire body tightened. "That punk gave up information on you? I'd kill him myself if he were still alive."

Emi's mind raced with everything she'd learned. Whatever it was hunting her was ruthless, and now it knew where she was. It also wanted to kill Lance.

She couldn't let that happen. No one else would die because of her.

Frantic, she stared around the room for clothing for Lance. She found a T-shirt, but that was it. She didn't think Taylor's shorts would fit Lance. Taylor was on the skinny side, and Lance could lift a house.

"We need to get Lance and get out of here. Like yesterday!" she yelled, running to the door—only to sense the dark energy she'd lived in fear of pushing in on her location quickly.

Austin stared around wildly, sheer terror coating his face. "He's coming, and he's not alone! He has these things. These monsters with him! Emi, you need to run!"

Hector caught her waist and stared in the direction of the front door. His entire body went rigid. "What the hell is that?"

"You feel it too?" She shouldn't have been that surprised. The evil that was barreling at them was so intense, she was sure everyone could sense it—even those who normally were immune to such things.

He nodded and curled his lip. "It feels like hundreds of bugs are crawling all over my skin."

"That would be the feel of pure evil," she said, turning and grabbing a discarded pair of Taylor's sweatpants. They would do in a pinch. She pushed on Hector. "You need to go out the back way and get as far from here as you can. Hurry!"

He shook his head. "Like hell. I'm not leaving you. Whatever is coming is really bad."

"Yeah! That would be why I'm telling you to get out of here," she said, nearly in a full-blown panic. Arguing with Hector was wasting precious time they didn't have. He needed to be far from the house and she had to get to Lance.

Hector put his hands out and fireballs appeared in both of his palms. "Not going to happen, Emi. Get to your new boy toy. I'll hold off whatever is coming."

She tugged on his shirt. "Hector, no! You can't hold it off. Trust me. I've been running from it since I was little. It killed my parents and my uncle. And it did a fine job of trying to kill three guys who make the Terminator look wimpy. We both should really get out of here. First, we need to get Lance."

"Emi?" Lance said from the top of the staircase.

There was a huge crashing sound from upstairs, and then snarls and growls. Abruptly, it sounded like an explosive had gone off up there. The house shook and there was a roar from above.

Then total silence.

Emi shrieked and rushed around Hector in an attempt to get to the back stairs. The entire time, she feared she'd see Lance's spirit, that he'd be dead.

253

She had to help Lance. It didn't matter that she'd seen just how capable he was when it came to fighting. Every fiber of her being demanded she be with him, fighting by his side against the threat.

She made it a few paces before the front door burst inward with such a force, it hit her hard enough to send her flying. The far wall stopped her when she collided with it, striking with enough force to momentarily cause her to black out. Pain radiated through her as she fell to the floor at the base of the steps.

"Emi!" yelled Hector and Fredrick at the same time, as Fredrick appeared out of thin air next to her.

The older man went to grab for her but his hand went through her body. That meant he'd expended a good deal of energy in trying to hold off the evil that was currently laying siege to the home.

"Emi, how badly are you injured?" demanded Fredrick.

She stifled a partial groan. "Got the wind knocked out of me. I think that's all. Is Lance dead?"

"No. Not yet," replied Fredrick, doing nothing to calm her already frantic state of mind.

There was a ball of orange light, and then something was on fire in the hallway with her. When she realized the burning something was one of the hybrid creatures, and that Hector had lit it up, she cried out, "No! Don't hurt them! They don't understand what they're doing. They can't help it."

Hector glanced at her, eyes wide, as if he couldn't believe she'd be on the side of the things attacking them.

Another creature charged from seemingly nowhere and struck Hector, knocking him through the wall, back into Taylor's room.

Emi pushed off the floor, ignoring the pain. She ran at the opening in the wall and looked at the creature. "Stop!"

It did, but it radiated hate and the need to feed. As it turned its attention to her, she realized it wasn't anything like Frank. It didn't have any redeeming qualities. Whoever it had been before it was turned into a hybrid creature, wasn't a good person. They'd been as disgustingly evil as the thing coming for her.

Hector lifted a hand and flames appeared. He glanced at Emi. "Tell me I can kill it."

"Carry on!" she yelled as one of the boarded-over windows behind Hector blew in. The debris just missed hitting Hector as he dove to the right and rolled on the floor, setting the creature on fire as he did. It ran through the halfway-open bedroom door and out into the night, the flames getting higher and higher as it did.

There was a loud hissing noise, and Emi glanced to the broken window to see what looked to be two blurs rushing through the opening.

It took a second for her eyes to adjust to the speed in which the attackers moved. They were hardly the clumsy yet brutal hybrids she'd seen so many of. These attackers were nimble, fast, and moved with a sleekness that was almost dancer-like, and incredibly deadly.

Hector glanced at her and they shared a look. She knew what he was intending to do, and she knew he was worried about hurting her, so she dove through the opening in the wall and rolled off to the side, just in time for Hector to unleash a lot of fire in the room.

Heat rolled through the opening at her. Once it finished, she got up, her intention to run back into the fray to help her friend in any way she could.

"This way!" shouted Fredrick as he pointed in the direction of the hallway, currently with no enemies in it.

She shook her head. "I can't leave Hector or Lance."

"They can handle themselves. Get out, Emi! Get out before *he* gets his hands on you and darkens your soul, too," Fredrick said, fear showing in his eyes.

"Listen to him, child!" said Mrs. Pumpernickel,

appearing quickly next to Fredrick and then vanishing.

Ignoring their warnings, Emi ran in the direction of Hector, hoping beyond hope that her friend was still alive and okay. While she understood he could create fire with his hands, she wasn't so sure he could withstand it to the degree she'd felt pouring from the room only moments before.

A second before she was about to reach the hole in the wall, something slammed into her from behind, knocking her to the floor as another giant ball of fire rolled out of the opening. This one whizzed above her head—right where she'd been standing.

For a split second, Emi thought the thing on top of her was Lance. Maybe even Hector.

It wasn't. It was the spirit in her house that she'd likened to evil. The dark one that caused so many issues. Why had it protected her?

She twisted around and stared at the mass of black mist. That was the only way it ever showed itself to her. The more she looked at it, the more it began to take shape before her very eyes—and what it morphed into stunned her.

"Uncle Yanko?" she asked, her voice barely there as reason escaped her.

Were her eyes playing tricks on her? Had hitting the wall left her with side effects that included hallucinations? Surely the dark entity in her home couldn't be her uncle. Could it?

It hit her then. The entity had never once hurt her. It had only kept others away and scared Taylor—someone her uncle wouldn't have been thrilled to have living with her. He would have thought Taylor was the type of guy who invited in trouble, and would've wanted Emi to stay far from him.

And the dark entity had done its best to get her to move away from the house. Away from New Orleans.

Always stay on the move, Emi.

Her uncle's words echoed in her head.

He stared down at her with eyes filled with moisture. A lone tear slid down his cheek. "Emi, get up and get away from here. Go! I can't keep him pinned for much longer."

"Uncle Yanko?" she asked once more, her heart racing. "What? How? Why?"

He sighed. "Emi, there isn't time for me to explain it all. You have to run! Get as far from here as you can. Chilton has found you."

Chilton?

Before she could question her uncle more on everything, he turned into black mist and went down through the floor in the direction of the never-used basement.

Emi scrambled to her hands and knees, hitting the floor, tears coming fast. "Uncle Yanko!"

He didn't come back.

As her mind began to clear, she turned and smelled smoke. The fireball that had come from Taylor's room had started a fire on the hallway wall. "Hector!"

She pushed to her feet and entered the room to find Hector there, throwing fire at two men who weren't creatures like Frank had been. They were vampires. And they certainly didn't look friendly. They looked like they wanted to make Hector their midnight snack.

The vampires snarled and leaped high in the air, just missing getting hit with Hector's fire.

"You're a hard one to find," said a man with a deep voice from behind her.

Turning, she found a man with gray eyes and pale skin that pulled at his face, making him look sickly. Death poured off him in a way that nearly made her gag, but he wasn't like Frank and the other creatures. He was something else.

In some ways, he was like Auberi and Blaise—the vampires she'd met—but that didn't feel right either. They didn't feel like death, and they didn't feel sinister. This guy did.

He's pure evil.

That was the difference, she realized. Auberi

and Blaise didn't radiate death, but they didn't exactly feel like rays of life, either. This man's aura was dark, threatening, and it made her want to shiver.

He reached for her, and she dodged his grasp, making the edges of his mouth draw up into a sneer. When he reached for her again, it was with a speed that stunned her. He grabbed her by the throat, his clawed fingers digging into her skin. The bite of pain made her eyes water, but she didn't cry.

She wouldn't give him the satisfaction.

"Emi!" yelled Hector, sounding as if he'd been slammed into the wall in Taylor's room.

Emi glared at the man holding her by the neck, refusing to show him fear. He was easy enough to read, letting her know he got off on hurting and scaring others. She wouldn't feed into his sick hunger.

He dragged her across the floor, closer to his thin frame. Lowering his head, he put his face close to hers and spoke, his breath smelling of old blood. "I don't know what the *new* master sees in you, but he wants you, so you're coming with me."

She batted at his arm, to no avail. "No," she managed.

He tightened his grip on her throat. "There could be an accident. You could be killed in the commotion."

Emi did the first thing she could think to do—she kneed the man in the balls.

He instantly released his hold on her throat and bent forward.

Happy to see kneeing was universally painful to men of all species, she spent a second rejoicing and then pushed him as hard as she could before letting her power build. The minute he looked up at her, baring hideous fangs and a contorted, demon-like face, she let her power go.

It slammed into him, knocking the vampire back from her and sending him hurtling down the hallway toward the open front door.

Emi rubbed her raw throat and blinked in surprise as a familiar face appeared behind the sinister vampire. Auberi grabbed hold of the man and yanked him off the floor, snarling as he did. The two vampires grabbed one another and took turns thrusting each other into the walls, making the house shake.

Someone grabbed her around the waist, and she reacted on instinct, kicking and elbowing. There was a loud groan, and then someone tapped her back gently.

"I…come…in…peace."

She spun around to find Blaise there, holding his groin. She gasped and reached for him.

He jerked back and held up a hand. "I surrender!"

"I'm sorry. I thought you were another vampire," she said before thinking better of it.

"I *am* another vampire," he said, still cupping himself, looking pained. "And I'm also a vampire who's going to need to have surgery from blunt testicular trauma."

"Yeah, well, you may be a smart-ass, but you're not evil like the other ones here." She touched his arm. "Sorry I elbowed you in your private parts."

He stilled. "Willing to kiss it and make it better?"

"I will elbow you again," she warned, his gaze sliding down.

He grinned and then stared past her as a huge cloud of dust seemed to suddenly coat the hall. He groaned. "Sure, Auberi, you had to kill a DustBuster one. I fucking hate those kinds of vamps. Better than the goo-guys, but messy as hell."

Goo-guys?

She wasn't sure she wanted to know.

Emi stared around, wondering where the gray-eyed vampire went. It took her a second to realize she was breathing him in as dust particles. She coughed. "Ohmygod, gross! Am I inhaling bad guy?"

"Yep," answered Blaise.

"Hold him!" shouted someone in Taylor's room.

Emi gasped. "Hector!"

Auberi motioned to Blaise. "Take Emi and go. I'll handle this."

"My friend is in there," said Emi sternly, refusing to budge.

"And would yer friend be the one who just threw fire at me?" asked a Scottish man as he came through the hole in the wall. He brushed down the front of his kilt, putting out the last bit of fire. "He's nae too happy right now with Daniel, who has him pinned to a mattress on the floor. But he was trying to ignite us all."

Auberi laughed. "No one would miss you. Well, no one but your mate, Searc."

Searc grinned. "You'd mourn me. Admit it."

"A little help in here, please," called a man who sounded very British.

"I'm nae getting near him again. He nearly burned off my family jewels," said Searc. "This is what we get for rushing over the second Toov does nae show at sunset. We get attacked by a human flamethrower."

Emi ran past the man in the kilt and Taylor's room to find Hector being pinned by a dark-haired man dressed in designer clothing. A tall, broad-shouldered man with ink-black hair was near them, laughing and taking a picture with his phone.

"Malik, what are you doing?" asked Auberi as he followed Emi into the room.

"The rest of the guys back at headquarters will want to see this," said the man with his phone out. "Could get him an honorable mention for Asshole of the Week."

Emi glanced around. "Where are the other two guys? The bad ones?"

Malik stopped taking pictures long enough to point to a pile of dust to the right of the room and a burned corpse to the left. "One is extra done, Pompeii style. The other one will need a broom and dustpan to collect all of him."

Emi exhaled in relief and then moved closer to the mattress on the floor. Taylor had never gotten around to finding a bed frame. She bent and touched her friend's shoulder. "Hector, please don't kill these guys. I think they're friends of my mate."

"Aye," said Searc. "Though he doesnae remember us verra much."

"I think he might now," Emi said, standing and helping Hector to his feet when the British guy got off him.

Malik chucked the British guy's shoulder. "Ha, Daniel, he took a lot of your energy to pin down."

Daniel leveled a hard gaze at Malik. "Thanks to all of your amazing assistance."

Malik laughed. "Hey, he was throwing fire at us.

I wasn't taking a chance on losing my eyebrows
—again."

The men all laughed.

Hector gave them all a hard look. "Emi, are you
sure I can't burn them all?"

"I'll think about it." Emi stared around at them.
"Where's Lance?"

They shared a look.

Auberi nodded to Blaise. "Get her out of here.
We'll find Toov."

"I'm not going anywhere without my mate," she
said firmly.

Malik lifted his head and sniffed the air. "I smell
another vampire."

"No shit," said Blaise. "There are how many of
us in the room right now? Get your kitty sniffer
checked. It's not working worth a damn."

Malik shook his head. "Not you guys, dipshit.
Another. A powerful one. There's a dark energy to
him. It's revolting."

Blaise gasped. "Chilton."

Emi didn't wait for the men. She took off
running in the direction of the back stairs. She
made it all the way up them and found Blaise hot on
her heels. She was about to run down the hall in the
direction of her room, where she'd last left Lance,
when Blaise grabbed her and leaped high in the air.

She cried out in surprise, and he landed,

pushing her against the wall before pointing to what used to be the floor.

It was gone, leaving only a huge hole in its place.

And clearly, someone large had fallen through it.

"Ohmygod, Lance!" she yelled, wiggling free from Blaise's hold and rushing in the direction of the hole in the floor. She stopped just before it and stared down...and down...and down.

Blaise did as well. "Holy shit. That goes all the way to the basement level."

"Lance!" she yelled down the hole.

"Toov? You alive?" called Blaise, snaking his arm around Emi's waist to keep her from falling.

There was no response.

Fear slammed into her, and she bent, yelling again. Blaise yanked her up and back as more of the floor gave in. Her heart went to her throat. She knew Lance was down there, and if her guess was right, so was the darkness that had been hunting her.

Austin appeared next to her, with Fredrick and Mrs. Pumpernickel at his side. Fredrick pointed to the hole in the floor. "Your husband is down there, with the ultimate evil. Lance is alive, but you have to hurry to him, Emi."

Mrs. Pumpernickel fanned her face with her hand. "Oh heavens. What a mess they've made. But, on the bright side, my jewelry is there for you, sweet child. My no-good son did not get it. You take it all. I want you to have it."

"W-what?" asked Emi, not following. "Husband? Lance isn't my husband. He didn't claim me."

Blaise put his face to her neck and breathed in deep. "Uh, yeah he did. You're mated to Amnesia-Boy."

"I will push you down the hole," she cautioned.

He grinned. "I really like you."

Chapter Twenty

"LANCE?"

"Toov? You alive?"

Thor blinked, and darkness surrounded him. Disoriented, he tried to sit up but realized he was pinned under something substantial. His brain scrambled to figure out what had happened. The last thing he remembered was putting on his jeans, unconcerned with the dried blood on them, and going in search of Emi and her buddy who had shown up. It was then he'd sensed dark power moving over the area, and he'd smelled Chilton fast approaching.

He gasped, remembering that he'd been at the top of the stairs when a boarded-over window had suddenly burst in at him, bringing with it, Chilton.

The two men had locked together and, in the next breath, the floor had given out from under them.

That was all he could remember.

Thor felt around, trying to figure out what was on him and why everything was so dark. As his hands moved over bricks, he groaned. Not only had he fallen through the floor, he'd apparently had bricks spill onto him as well.

Why the fuck not?

He shoved the mass of bricks and debris from him and made a move to rise, only to find something was sticking through his stomach. He felt around and let out an annoyed breath. A piece of wood had impaled him. Taking hold of it, he clenched his jaw and then yanked the wood free, groaning as he did.

Sure, it hurt, but Chilton was in the home—and so was Emi. It didn't matter what kind of damage he'd sustained, he had to protect his mate.

Finally free from the wood, he managed to stand, only to sway and nearly fall again.

He reached out and steadied himself with the wall—a second before the debris around him exploded up and out with such a force, the wall Thor had his hand on gave way. He tumbled with the sliding rock and twisted around just in time to catch Chilton before the vampire would have snapped his neck.

Thor held the vampire at bay, shifting partially into hybrid form. He used the added strength to thrust Chilton from him. He then came up as if on strings, his claws out, his fangs distended. He was ready to kill the enemy.

No games.

No playtime.

Chilton came up quickly as well, his long dark hair falling partially into his face. A face that seemed tanned year-round. Chilton hunched his shoulders, his own nails lengthening. "You dared to touch her?"

Thor stepped around the rubble and walked in a circle, keeping his eyes on the enemy, ready for the attack. This confrontation had been a long time coming, and he was more than ready to kill the asshole.

"You dared to think you could put your filthy shifter hands upon my daughter?" demanded Chilton.

Daughter?

The question threw Thor for a loop.

Hesitating, he stared at the man harder, instantly noting the similarities between the man he hated and Emi. The same eyes. The same skin tone. They even had the same lip shape and hair color.

No.

It couldn't be.

Gasping, Thor shook his head. Emi said the darkness killed her parents. She never mentioned her father *was* the fucking darkness.

Chilton snarled. "I will make your death painful and slow."

Thor put a hand up, needing answers before he killed the man. "Hold the phone here, asshole. What do you mean, your *daughter*? Emi can't be yours."

Could she?

Chilton was dressed as he normally was, in what could only be called a pirate shirt and a pair of black leather pants. He was pretty much what everyone thought of when they pictured a vampire —and seemed to take fashion advice from Pierre. A total dick with an obsession with leather and a penchant for fashion that was woefully outdated.

He lifted his chin in defiance. "I can smell her scent on you. You defiled her!"

Seven times, thought Thor, but didn't voice as much. Besides, he'd hadn't defiled her. He'd made love to her. To *his* woman—and he wouldn't let the Dracula wannabe cheapen what he had with his mate.

"She's my mate, so back the fuck off the 'defile' remarks, dickhead," said Thor, ready to kill the man and end his mindfuck.

Chilton drew back slightly, disbelief in his eyes. "Your mate?"

Thor nodded. "And if you try to hurt her, I'll tear your head off and send it back to Gérard gift wrapped."

Chilton puffed out his chest, clearly posturing. "Gérard is no more. *I* am the master now."

"Gérard is dead?" asked Thor. That was news to him, and he knew damn well Pierre didn't know, either.

Chilton grinned, the look in his eyes nothing short of crazy. "I killed him myself. He was weak. He didn't deserve to rule. It was simply a matter of time before Pierre seized the territory, so I beat him to it. I'm the master of these parts now. All will bow to me."

Yep. Totally crazy.

The more Thor thought about it, the angrier he became. "Hold on. That means you're who sent those hybrids after Emi and me. Dick move! If she's supposedly your kid, why the hell would you try to kill her?"

"They were sent to kill *you* and retrieve my daughter," said Chilton.

"Seriously, stop with the daughter thing. That can't be."

"Yet it is. Her mother was my mate. Gérard forbid

me from seeing her, and even tried to kill her and my child when he learned the truth of it all. I went to stop it from happening. I was too late. I arrived just as Yanko came. And he blamed me for his sister's death. He took Emanaia far from my reach and kept her hidden. It took me years to track them down; each time I got close, Yanko would run with her again. Finally, I saw to it he could run no more. But my daughter had learned too much from him. She ran on her own. It took me years to locate her once more."

Thor stared at the man. "I feel pretty comfortable in saying she's not going to be okay with who you are to her."

Chilton laughed maniacally. "She will have no choice. The time has come for her to return to me. We will rule Louisiana together. As we were meant to. Father and daughter, together again. Yanko can no longer stop me. And you will not live long enough to be a problem—*shifter*."

"Father and daughter?" Emi's voice echoed through the darkness as light burst into the area from above.

Lance looked up to find Emi standing in the open doorway at the top of the old wooden staircase leading to the basement. Blaise and Auberi were next to her.

Chilton grinned, his eyes widening. "Emanaia, darling."

Emi jerked as Chilton spoke.

A large black mass appeared between Thor and Chilton. It took the shape of a tall man with a head of closely cut dark hair.

Had Thor finally gone mad? Had a figure really just appeared out of thin air?

"Uncle Yanko!" yelled Emi from above.

Yanko? As in the dead guy?

Oh goodie, now I'm seeing the dead too.

Chilton snarled, staring around the room wildly. "I can sense you. Where are you, coward?"

"I am no coward, Chilton," said the figure as it swayed, like a breeze was blowing it lightly. "I will not allow you to harm her."

"Is he really my father?" asked Emi, emotions written across her face.

Yanko glanced up at her, pain on his face.

Chilton gazed around, looking like a feral dog. "Where are you?"

Thor glanced from Emi to Yanko. "Why is it I'm seeing you?"

Yanko offered a half smile. "Because you claimed my niece. Your system took a bit to adjust to the new gift, but it is there, and will forever be there."

Thor tensed. "I didn't claim Emi. In fact, I made a point *not* to claim her."

Yanko grunted. "Then consider yourself an epic

failure in that department. Now, if you would be so kind as to keep that madman away from Emi…"

"Not a problem," said Thor, his attention moving to Chilton. "I don't care who he is to her, he's not touching her."

Emi shook her head. "He can't be my father. My father died in a fire when I was little. He died with my mother. He killed them!"

Chilton hissed. "Lies that Yanko told you."

"No," she whispered.

Yanko sighed. "Emi, he speaks the truth. I tried to hide it from you. I thought it would be too much for you at such a young age—to know your father was not only a creature of the night, but a man who killed for pleasure."

Auberi grabbed Emi as she tried to come down the stairs. "No, Emi. Chilton's mind is broken," said Auberi. "Blaise and I can sense it upon him. He's not only drinking blood, he's eating the flesh of his own kind. That makes a vampire's mind snap quickly."

Thor's stomach churned at the idea of anyone eating vampire. The fact Chilton had resorted to cannibalism to gain power shouldn't have shocked him. The man had never been right in the head.

Chilton spit as he shouted, "Lies! All lies to twist my daughter against me! Come, my beautiful Emanaia. We will be a family together!"

Emi stared at Auberi. "Can you sense if he's really my father?"

Blaise touched her shoulder. "Yes. The vampire side of you is so faint, we both would have missed it had we not smelled you and Chilton in the same room. And then there's the fact you can control the Franken-beasts. Like a master vampire would be able to do."

Auberi grunted. "Chilton is no master."

Thor cleared his throat. "He killed Gérard."

"This is not good," said Auberi. "Toov, he is far too broken to be permitted to live."

Yanko nodded. "It is true. His mind went long ago, before he fully mated to my sister. Before he left Emi growing within my sister's body. The death of my sister pushed him over the edge of reason—not that her death had far to shove him. The small piece of humanity he'd retained back then died the same day she did. From that point forward, he has only grown into a darker evil. One that cannot not be permitted to continue onward."

Thor's mind raced with the repercussions of killing Chilton. "He's Emi's father. If I kill him, she'll die."

Blaise lifted a brow. "Since when?"

"Pierre explained in detail how it all works! A sire, either blood or biological, holds the lifeline of all those under him," said Thor, wanting to gut

Chilton but fearing for Emi. "A direct connection like father and daughter, or a blood bond, means they're tied. Bound to one another. Like I'm bound to Pierre and will die without his blood."

"Bullshit!" yelled Blaise. "Fuck him up. She'll be fine. My brother is a liar. He needs you to obey, and the only way to do that is by forcing his blood on you. You'll need blood to live, but you can feed from your mate, or live off bagged shit. Your choice."

What?

Could it be true?

Could he be free of Pierre and get to keep his mate?

His moment of jubilation was cut short as Chilton charged him, hitting him in his midriff and lifting him into the air. The pair collided with the brick wall and the entire home shook. Chilton sank his fangs deep into Thor's neck and attempted to tear his head back, taking Thor's neck with him.

Thor grabbed hold of his head and held him there. He was about to snap the man's neck when, all of a sudden, Chilton was ripped free by an unseen force.

Vaguely, Thor heard Auberi and Blaise yelling for Emi.

Worry cut through him.

He looked over to see Emi near him, her arms out wide, her eyes fully black, like a vampire's would be when their demon was in control. But he didn't sense a demon in her. Only dark magik.

She stared at Chilton. "Are you really beyond redemption?"

The vampire hissed and tried to lunge at Emi. Thor reacted, ripping Chilton back and keeping him from harming her. Some father the asshole was. From the way he fought against Thor's hold, he intended to kill his own daughter.

Thor would not allow that to happen.

He raised his clawed hand toward Chilton's throat. A second before he attacked, Yanko was there, thrusting Thor from Chilton.

Yanko stopped looking solid and actually went into Chilton's body.

Stunned by what he was seeing, Thor simply stood there, mouth agape.

Emi remained where she was, arms out, chanting softly in what he could only guess was Latin.

Chilton fell to the floor—and then burst into a pile of ash.

Yanko rose up from the ashes, reforming into a man, his gaze on Thor. "Stop her! She calls upon all of Chilton's creations. The creatures who hunt the streets. She is summoning them here so they can harm no others."

"W-what?" asked Thor in stunned surprise. "She's calling the hybrids here? How?"

"They were gifted to Gérard, and he fed them his blood to keep them enthralled. When he perished by Chilton's hand, Chilton took over feeding them—controlling them."

Thor gasped. "And because Emi is his daughter, she shares his bloodline. That's why she could control Frank?"

"Frank?" asked Yanko.

Thor held up his hand. "Long story. How do I stop her?"

"Shit! There are a whole lot of hybrids showing up!" yelled Blaise. "Tell your woman to stop whispering to them. They're coming in numbers we're going to have issues with."

"Emi, sweetheart, stop," said Thor, moving toward her.

She didn't budge or acknowledge him.

He touched her shoulder. "Emi, I can feel how much energy this is taking from you. Stop before you hurt yourself."

He ignored the commotion from above. The PSI guys would do what needed to be done in regards to the hybrids. His only worry was his mate.

She kept whispering the chant, her arms still out.

"Emi, stop," he said again, before dragging her into his embrace. "Enough."

She shook in his arms. "My father is responsible for them. For the deaths they've caused. For so much pain. I have to stop it. I have to stop them."

"Not at a cost to yourself," Thor said. He took hold of her chin and forced her face upward. "Woman, I didn't go through hell and back and end up some crazy vampire's lapdog, all to watch the woman I love sacrifice herself because she feels guilty her biological father was a nutcase. He's dead and gone now, Emi. The man who raised you like a daughter wasn't like him. You told me Yanko was important to you."

"He was." She teared up. "He still is."

"He's like a father to you, not Chilton," said Thor, running his thumb over his mate's lower lip. "And he just made sure Chilton could never harm you again. I'd say that is a big fucking gesture of just how much you mean to him. He transcended death to protect you."

She cried harder. "Turns out he's been haunting my house for years."

Thor laughed slightly. "So, what you're saying is, my in-law is going to give me a hard time for, like, ever?"

She smiled through her tears. "Yes."

"Sweetheart, stop drawing the hybrids here," he said softly.

"They were told to go out and kill as many humans as they could. I can sense the directive on them. I had to summon them here." She closed her eyes a moment, and then opened them. The black was gone. "I'm sorry. But they couldn't be allowed to kill people."

"Son of a bitch!" yelled Blaise from above. "That hurt!"

"Sorry!" said Hector. "I didn't know you'd be standing so close to it when I lit it on fire."

Thor hid his laughter. While they'd have their hands full, they would come out victorious. He knew it deep down. He bent his head and pressed his lips to his wife's mouth—and then froze.

My wife?

He gasped against her mouth. "I claimed you."

She smiled. "I heard."

"That means we're mated. We're husband and wife."

She snorted. "Yeah, heard that too."

"And now you're going to go assist your friends while I spend time with my niece," said Yanko sternly, reminding Thor they weren't alone.

Emi took hold of Thor's hand. "Uncle Yanko, I want to introduce you to my husband. His name is Lance, but he goes by Thor."

Thor took a deep breath. "Actually, I'd like to be called Lance."

Emi squealed and threw her arms around his neck. "That a boy, Lance!"

He heard Searc shouting at Daniel and knew he should go up and help the men out, but he didn't want to let go of his mate. "Pretty sure I need to lend a hand up there."

Emi winked and took his hand in hers, turning his hand palm side up. "Hurry, and then we need to make sure Hector is going to watch Rocky while we're in Virginia."

"Virginia?" asked Lance.

Emi nodded. "We're heading there after you kill all the bad guys. We're going to meet up with your family—the men you think of as brothers. They're there now, pacing, worried about you. They wanted to come but the men here said no. They'd bring you home to them."

Lance watched his woman. "You got all that from my palm?"

"Some from you and some from when Blaise touched me. He's like an open book. And really, can I just say, he should talk to a professional. If you knew some of the weird thoughts that guy had, you'd all sleep with one eye open."

Lance kissed her forehead, his gut churning at the idea of going home to his Immortal Ops team.

Emi hugged him. "It will be fine. They've missed you, Lance. They love you and want you back with them. And they're going to be really good uncles."

"Uncles?" he asked.

Emi glanced to the side, and a middle-aged woman appeared, dressed in clothing from the past. She was plump and grinning.

"I wondered if you'd see your own future when reading his," said the woman.

Lance gasped at the sight of her.

Emi laughed. "Lance, meet Mrs. Pumpernickel."

The woman winked and then raked her gaze over him. "You have the best backside."

Lance blushed.

The woman pointed to the rubble at the back of the basement. "Emi, while your handsome husband goes up to handle the bad men, go over there and get my jewelry. Take it all with you. I want you to have it. You're like family to me."

Lance glanced at Yanko, who was giving him the stink eye. "I'm never going to get used to seeing dead people."

Emi laughed. "Sure you will."

Lance thought about what she'd said about his teammates. "Hold on. What do you mean, they'll make good uncles?" His gaze slid down and landed on her abdomen. "You're pregnant?"

"I will be soon," she said with a wide smile. "Well, only if you hurry up and get on with killing the enemy. Then we can get to Virginia and get busy in other ways."

Lance bent and kissed her quickly and then rushed for the stairs. He was halfway up them when he heard his mate's laughter behind him.

"Well, I guess that's one way to motivate the boy," said Yanko.

Chapter Twenty-One

EMI HELD her husband's hand as they were led through the halls of what they'd been told was Immortal Ops Headquarters. A voice came through speakers mounted throughout the building. It was pleasant sounding enough, but what it spoke of was anything but. It gave a casualty update and mission report from something that happened overseas. Her gut churned as she thought about the lost lives of the soldiers and the loved ones who would be left without them.

Lance lifted their joined hands and kissed her knuckles, one by one. "Sweetheart, it's an automated system that keeps us informed on missions from every branch of the military, both US and ally forces."

"It's heartbreaking to hear," she confessed.

He nodded. "I know. Some days are like that. But it's important we hear about it all. The good and the bad. The men and women fighting out there may not know us, but we worry about them. We want them safe and their missions to be a success."

She leaned against him, happy he could remember so much from his past. The private flight in had been comical, to say the least, as they'd been accompanied by Auberi, Blaise, Daniel, Searc, and Malik. They'd been delayed at takeoff for a bit as bad weather blew through New Orleans, but once they were in the air, Auberi went to the fully stocked wet bar and began mixing drinks for everyone. As the liquor flowed, so did the questions. The other men wanted to know what all that Lance could remember from his time before a man they'd called Pierre had come into his life—or rather death.

Emi didn't know much about Pierre other than the fact he seemed like a giant tool and that none of the men cared for him. Auberi and Blaise especially seemed to want his head mounted on their walls. She'd gotten the gist of Pierre being a master vampire, one who'd had Lance under his thumb for a good deal of time. And one Lance wanted to exact revenge upon. From the sounds of it, Lance would have to line up after Auberi and Blaise to get his pound of flesh.

Emi squeezed her mate's hand when she felt him tensing as they continued to walk down the long hallway. The building and the facility looked state of the art to her. Like something she'd seen in a science fiction movie, and it was certainly a far cry from the run down, abandoned house she'd called home.

Lance let out a low breath. He was nervous, and she could tell. She couldn't blame him. From what she'd gathered on the plane ride to Virginia, the men they were about to see had not just been fellow teammates to him. They'd been like family to Lance. And for a chunk of time, they'd thought he was dead, only to find out he was alive, part-vampire, and working for Pierre with no memories of his past.

Of before he crossed over the threshold of death.

Blaise and Auberi walked ahead of them, each taking turns mocking the décor at the I-Ops head-quarters, all the while comparing it to the PSI offices. Apparently, they thought PSI was better. She wasn't sure how that could be, but they seemed sure of it.

"Where is he?" someone yelled from behind them. A tall man with black shoulder-length hair ran past Malik, Searc, and Daniel. The man came to a grinding halt, his blue gaze widening. He had on a pair of faded jeans that fit him just right and a pink T-shirt that was snug, pulling over his muscles. Apparently, he was the world's best father, as noted by his shirt. "L-Lance?"

Lance didn't budge. He merely stared at the man and clutched Emi's hand in a death grip. "Hey, Roi."

Emi hid her smile as she remembered the crash course on the men she'd received from Lance before landing. Geoffroi "Roi" Majors was second in command of the I-Ops team, and often something of a pain in the ass, and who had a thing for the ladies. Blaise had mentioned Roi was mated to a woman named Missy and that they had twin girls. That only made the shirt funnier, knowing the alpha male had two little girls at home.

Roi flashed a wide smile that lit up the hall. "Aww, I knew they were all full of shit when they said you forgot us. See, you may have forgotten everyone else, but I'd like to think I make a lasting impression."

"Yeah, you could say that," said a man with white-blond hair as he strolled in from other direction. "Try as I might, I can't forget you. And you should know, I try really fucking hard every day."

"Who invited you to the party, Eadan?" asked Roi, looking annoyed. "Fae's aren't welcome."

Lance hadn't said much about him. It had been

Malik who had filled in the blanks on that team member, mentioning that Eadan Daly had come on board after Lance's departure to assist the I-Ops and was now a full-fledged member of the team.

"Then Emi will need to leave," said Malik, staring between the men. "I can smell hints of it on her. Well, and I can smell Lance's claim on her too."

Emi perked. She had Fae in her? She wasn't even entirely sure what Fae was, but she knew she'd find out soon enough.

"We thought you were dead, Lance." Roi looked like he was about to tear up. Instead, he lowered his head and rubbed his eyes. "Fucking rag weed count is high. My, uh, allergies are acting up."

Eadan snorted. "Mr. Sensitive here is all in touch with his feelings and shit."

"Is he here yet?" asked a man with close cut brown hair and a couple of days' worth of growth on his face.

Eadan nodded in Lance's direction. "Yes, and he's barely shut up. Kidding. I don't think he speaks."

Lance looked at the newcomer, and a lopsided smile appeared on his face. "Wilson."

Wilson beamed and rushed Lance, pulling him into a giant hug, seemingly unconcerned with the fact he was showing emotion. Lance released Emi's hand and returned Wilson's embrace. Wilson drew back and patted Lance's shoulders. "We missed you, brother."

"You can say that again," said a man with long, wavy dark brown hair. His blue gaze was so similar to Roi's that Emi wondered if they were brothers. "It's really good to have you home, Lance."

Lance stiffened and then nodded, looking as if he were fighting the urge to cry. "Lukian."

Lukian Vlakhusha covered the distance between them quickly and did a manly version of a hug with Lance as well. He drew back and kept an arm over Lance's shoulder. "Heads up, Green is scrambling to get all the tests he wants to run on you in order."

Emi hid her grin. Lance had told her of Dr. Green and how he prided himself on putting science before nearly everything in life. He also said that he shared panther DNA with Green, making him closer to an actual brother to him than the rest of the team.

Roi composed himself, kind of, and strolled over to them. "It's his way of saying he missed you. The egghead can't help but bring science in to cover his feelings."

"Unlike using the allergies excuse?" asked Eadan.

"Captain, permission to kill Eadan," said Roi with an even look on his face.

Lukian sighed. "No. I've already told you, you can't kill him."

"Please."

Wilson laughed. "At least he's finally stopped begging to kill me."

Another man entered the hallway, and everyone grew quiet, backing up, making room for him despite the hall being quite large. The man had close cut sandy blond hair and amber eyes. A wash of emotions covered his handsome face as he locked gazes with Lance.

Lance teared up. "Jon?"

Jon rushed him, and the men collided with a thud, hugging and turning in a circle, each hitting the other on the back as the tears flowed. Jon took Lance's hand in his and then held their joined hands, much like they were about to arm wrestle in midair. "I shouldn't have let them take you. I should have realized you weren't dead. I'm so fucking sorry."

Emi couldn't stop herself as she stepped forward. "He did die. And from the sounds of it all, you couldn't have known what they were planning."

Jon glanced at Lance and lifted a brow. "You did die?"

Lance nodded. "I'm not really clear on what all happened after Parker attacked. I remember waking up with Pierre above me and I could hear Krauss's voice, though I didn't know who Krauss was then."

Jon gasped. "I'm sorry, brother."

Lance hugged him again. "I think it was meant to be."

Jon drew back, looking unsure.

Lance released the man and put his hand out to Emi. She went to him at once and he drew her against his powerful frame. "Had events not unfolded the way they did, I don't think I'd have found Emi—my mate. I may have lived through hell, but I'm so fucking happy right now, Jon. I found what we always thought was a myth. I found the woman made for me. And I hear you guys all found your special someone's too."

As those words left his lips, Emi couldn't help but look toward Auberi, Blaise, Malik, Searc, and Daniel. Only Searc was mated out of the men they'd flown in with.

Auberi caught her watching him and froze. "No. Do not look at me with pity. I am quite happy single."

Blaise licked his lips. "I like a different woman nightly. Keeps things interesting."

"Och, you say that now, but when you meet yer mate, you cannae imagine ever taking another," said Searc.

Daniel remained oddly quiet on the matter.

Malik glanced away, as if the topic pained him. Maybe it did.

Jon stared at Lance. "You're okay then?"

"What he means to say is, we heard you've got vamp in you which totally blows," said Wilson, pointing to the vampires among them. "Case in point."

"Asshole," said Blaise.

Auberi flashed fang at Wilson.

Daniel merely looked at him as if he made him tired.

Searc paid him no mind.

Lance laughed. "I'm good. I'll admit it was touch and go for a bit there. I thought my mind was breaking. Turns out I was breaking Pierre's hold on me. I think meeting Emi is what finally did it. I love her so much and honestly, we only just found one another."

"Works for me." Jon smiled wide and came for Emi, swooping her out of Lance's embrace and lifting her high in the air before hugging her.

The next thing she knew, Lukian had her and was hugging her too. "Thank you for being there for him."

She wasn't able to respond before Wilson had her and was hugging her too. "Welcome to the family. Heads up, we're totally dysfunctional."

"Speak for yourself, rat," said Roi, snatching

Emi out of Wilson's hold and hugging her. He trembled when he did and she realized he was crying silently. He bent his head, shielding it from the other men.

Emi turned her face and pretended to sneeze. "Darn ragweed."

Roi gathered his composure and winked at her, mouthing the word "thanks".

"Stop hogging her," said another man, this one tall with auburn hair and emerald green eyes. He had on a lab coat and was finishing up hugging Lance. He stepped back, his gaze going to Emi. "Good luck escaping this motley crew."

Emi smiled wide, feeling like she was already part of their family.

Lance glanced around. "Where is Colonel Brooks?"

Lukian sighed. "He took off out of here three days back, refusing to let any of us go with him. Said he has a lead on a supposed second I-Ops team."

"As if," snorted Wilson. "We're elite and the only ones."

Lance rubbed the back of his head. "Uh, about that."

Roi frowned. "Do not tell me the government started up testing again. Didn't they learn with all of us and the Outcasts?"

Emi tipped her head. "Outcasts?"

Wilson sighed. "Men who didn't come out totally right from the other side of the testing the government did to create us."

"Good men that our government turned on," said Jon sternly.

Lance's lips drew into a thin line. "We weren't the only successful manufactured team of supernatural operatives assembled."

"Yes, we were," argued Roi.

"Enough with all the downer stuff. Our wives are looking after our little ones because they wanted us to be able to spend time with you. We can talk about all the depressing stuff later." Wilson licked his lips. "Okay, let's drink. Then we can grill Lance and find out all the stupid shit Pierre dressed him in. I saw this one guy who was rumored to be linked to the vampire and he was in a dog collar and nothing else. Tell me, did you sport that look while there?"

"Where is a dart gun when you need it?" asked Lance, making his teammates share a look before they all converged on him, lifting him in the air, laughing.

Emi laughed as Malik eased up alongside her. He put his arm around her. "He'll be fine now."

"What about the Pierre guy?" she asked.

Auberi came to a stop on her other side. "We'll

handle him. Lance's place is near you, not out hunting a madman."

Malik gave her a good squeeze. "You're going to fit in great here. I heard it through the grapevine that Jon's wife can also see and hear the dead."

"Really?" Emi asked, excited to meet someone else like her. Since Yanko had passed she'd been very alone when it came to what she could do. Sure, Lance could do it now too, but he was so new to it that it freaked him out.

Lance bent as the men took turns playfully punching him in the stomach. Men were very odd and had strange ways of showing affection for one another. Emi watched their antics and found she couldn't stop smiling.

Suddenly, she felt something close to her— something no longer of the living.

Turning, she spotted her uncle there, grinning as he leaned against the wall. "These are good men, Emi. You'll be happy here. Now, tell your mate it's time to work on a family. The perfect window of opportunity is upon you both."

Emi gasped. "Uncle Yanko, I'm not going to tell Lance that if he wants a baby, he has to jump my bones right now."

Everyone turned to stare at her and she realized that she'd just announced her uncle's idea to the entire group. She blushed.

Lance moved away from his team fast, his eyes wide and on Yanko. "Seriously?"

Her uncle nodded.

"Uh, who is Lance talking to?" asked Roi.

"Oh, dude, he's got residual creepy vampire mojo going on," said Wilson, earning him a slap in the back of the head from Lukian. "What? He didn't used to talk to thin air."

Jon snorted. "He's talking to a dead person."

"Wait?" asked Emi, realizing Jon was staring right at her uncle. "You can see him too?"

Jon nodded.

Emi smiled. "I'm really going to love it here."

Lance grabbed her and lifted her off her feet. "Captain, permission to use one of the extra sleeping quarters here until I can get a home of my own set up. I need to get to work making a baby. From what Malik told me, I've got some catching up to do with you guys. You're like baby making machines."

The men smiled.

Lukian pushed Jon slightly. "Tell him."

Jon groaned. "You don't have to get a new place. We kind of kept your old one. Okay, well, we sold it, but it bothered us so we bought it back. It doesn't have furniture in it, but then again, you had shit taste in furniture so it's for the best."

Lukian leaned. "And yes, go grab a sleeping

quarter and make yourself at home. We'll see to it your home has everything the two of you need."

Blaise waggled his brows. "Can I watch while you guys go start on the family?"

Lance growled.

Emi laughed. "Stop. He's just being him."

"Can I kill him?"

"After you make love to me," she said, kissing his cheek. "I love you, Lance."

"I love you too, sweetheart."

"Aww, that is so sweet that I have a fang ache from it," said Blaise, a second before Lance ran after him.

"Boys," Emi huffed, shaking her head as her husband tackled Blaise to the floor.

THE END

About the Author

Dear Reader

Did you enjoy this title and want to know more about Mandy M. Roth, her pen names and all the titles she has available for purchase (over 100)?

About Mandy:

New York Times & *USA TODAY* Bestselling Author Mandy M. Roth is a self-proclaimed Goonie, loves 80s music and movies and wishes leg warmers would come back into fashion. She also thinks the movie The Breakfast Club should be mandatory viewing for...okay, everyone. When she's not dancing around her office to the sounds of the 80s or writing books, she can be found designing book covers for New York publishers, small presses, and indie authors.

Learn More:

To learn more about Mandy and her pen names, please visit http://www.mandyroth.com

For latest news about Mandy's newest releases and sales subscribe to her newsletter

http://www.mandyroth.com/newsletter/

To join Mandy's Facebook Reader Group: The Roth Heads, please visit

https://www.facebook.com/groups/Mandy-RothReaders/

Review this title:

Please let others know if you enjoyed this title. Consider leaving an honest review on the vendor site in which you purchased this title. Reviews help to spread the word and boost overall sales. This means more books in the series you love.

Thank you!

Want to see what other books Mandy has out? Visit her website!

www.mandyroth.com

Made in the USA
Monee, IL
28 June 2022

98750434R00187